ALL WE NEED IS LOVE

Stories of devotion, desire, and the *full catastrophe*

Patsy Trench

© Prefab Publications 2021

Published in 2021
by Prefab Publications, London

ISBN 978-0-9934537-6-2

Cover image by Michael Burge

*True love is like ghosts, which everyone
talks about and few have seen.*

François de La Rochefoucauld

Contents

The non-love song

I'm not going to sing a love song,
'Cos love songs are kind of boring.
Sentimental displays
Of age-old clichés
There's nothing that's not been said before,
in
Fact. It

Wouldn't be quite so bad if
Lovers were better at it.
For it's when something goes wrong
That they burst into song,
As if we should care – so what?
So what? It

Isn't the end, and
You're not really dying,
Let go of my shoulder,
It's not there to cry on.
My heart is intact and my nerves are okay,
I sleep well at night and I'm happy this
way.

Talk until doomsday
I'm not going to listen
To you losing your mind
And your sense of proportion.

How could I sing a love song?
I don't even know what love is.
For despite all those millions
Of torch songs and sonnets,
Heart-rending stanzas
From miserable poets,
No matter how often
They sing it or rhyme it,
Nobody seems to know how to define it.

That's why
I'm not going to sing a love song.
Because love is a myth
That only exists
In lovers' imaginations.

Introduction

John met Jackie one day in the park. They were sitting side by side on a bench watching people feeding the ducks and they got chatting and discovered they had things in common. They exchanged numbers and met up again a couple of times and got to really like one another. On the third meeting John told Jackie he wanted to sleep with her, at which point Jackie paused for a moment and said, 'Do you love me?'

There was another pause before John said, 'I thought we could have dinner beforehand – I know this great little Greek place on . . .'

'I said do you love me?' Jackie repeated.

There was yet another short pause and then John said, 'Yes'.

'Then say it.'

'I love you,' said John.

'Do you mean it?'

'I love you,' said John again, with meaning.

'Or are you only saying it because I asked you to?'

There was a definite hiatus while John attempted to hide his exasperation, and then he said, 'What do you mean by love anyway?'

That's where our eavesdropping ends, before Jackie gets to answer the million dollar question. Because the point is Jackie was me, or you, as there were times in my life as there may have been in yours when it seemed vitally important to introduce the word 'love' into a relationship, not least because way back when it was considered beyond the pale to sleep with anyone unless it was for love.

~

What *does* the word 'love' mean, anyway? If all we need for a peaceful and happy world is to love one another, why don't we simply do so? Why do we have to complicate it? If love conquers all why don't we just sit back and wallow in love?

The answer is that love, like truth, is 'rarely pure and never simple', to borrow from Oscar Wilde. It's not just singers who croon about love gone wrong. Most classic tales of love are of love forbidden (*Abelard and Heloise, Romeo & Juliet*), or withheld (*Dido & Aeneas, Medea & Jason*). True, Elizabeth Bennet gets her man eventually, as does Jane Eyre. But the world has it in for Cathy and Heathcliff, not to mention Anna Karenina and Jay Gatsby. In the real world William Hazlitt's love for his landlord's daughter Sarah nearly drove him mad, and of course Wilde's 'love that dare not speak its name' for Bosie was not just illicit and mostly unreciprocated but led him to prison, disgrace and early death.

At the same time it wasn't love that did for Romeo and Juliet, it was tribal conflict going back so far nobody could remember the original cause. It was Jason's selfishness and Medea's justified jealousy that brought about their tragedy; and class and, again, jealousy, that kept Cathy and Heathcliff apart. Gatsby and Hazlitt were doomed by their obsession and Anna Karenina by her impulsive despair. Wilde's real enemy was not the law that disgraced him and put him in prison, it was his terrible choice of lover. There is certainly such a thing as too much love, or too little, and when you come to think of it the chances of both sides loving one another equally in order to create the perfect relationship are pretty slim.

Love is more than romantic love of course. The following stories, written over a period of around fifteen years and with one exception pre-Covid, are about love in various forms: familial love; love of a country or a belief; love of a people or a pet or a work of art; love between friends; love undemonstrated, as well as love withheld, unrequited or unwanted. Many of them are true, or based on truth. The one thing they have in common is that they demonstrate the belief that love is like a red red rose: beautiful, prickly and not always easy to find.

Young Claudia

My book 'The Awakening of Claudia Faraday' tells the tale of a fifty-something mother of three discovering the joys of sex for the first time. Here is my speculative account, set in the 1880s, of Claudia's early days experimenting with love when she was what we now term a teenager.

She did so long to fall in love. She'd read about it, in novels mostly, for how else does a young girl get to hear about such a thing? Certainly not from her mother. Her friends claimed to know all about it, but when she asked them to expand there was some shrugging and sighing and, 'I can't really describe it, you just know it when it happens, and it's rather marvellous really.'

'Rather marvellous really' sounded good enough to Claudia, and so it was with high expectations that she set out on her quest to fall in love.

She was an attractive girl. No, more, she was beautiful, even at that young age. She had the ideal mix of beauty and lack of self-awareness that rendered her irresistible. Try as she did to appear reserved, following strict instruction from her mother, her unbridled eagerness and impatience shone through all attempt at pretence.

Claudia could remember finding love perfectly easy as a child. She loved their dog Muffin. She loved the sunshine as it fell on the daffodils in the early days of spring. She loved strawberries. She loved it when her father was home and played blind man's buff with her, preferably when her mother was not around. She loved her father, though not always. She loved her mother too, if only because she was her mother, even if at times she didn't like her particularly.

Falling in love however was not the same, Claudia knew that. Handsome men turned out often to be vain and self-regarding, and even cruel. She had an instinctive mistrust of any young man who made sheep's eyes at her, or kissed her hand and held onto it for too long. Where was the challenge in that?

Her first contender was therefore an unlikely choice: a young man who wore spectacles, which Claudia thought gave him distinction, and tripped over steps, and stammered whenever he spoke to her – though oddly not at any other time – and whose name was George. She was attracted by his vulnerability and his constant air of bewilderment, and the curious way his spectacles bounced up and down on his nose when he sneezed (which he also did whenever he saw her). Here was the challenge she was looking for: as is it not the case that the first thing a girl likes to do when they fall in love with a man is change him?

To say this did not turn out quite as Claudia expected is not to say she did not enjoy the game. Having encouraged George to the point where he no longer sneezed when he saw her, and stammered only occasionally, Claudia found herself at a loss. Inexplicably her new beau had lost a good deal of his charm. It seemed she was a victim of her own success; for as everyone knows, in the unlikely event that a woman who sets out to change a man achieves her aim, whatever affection she felt for him originally is likely to turn to disdain for a man who allows a woman to manipulate him. Thus it was that the game being over and done with Claudia felt there was nowhere left to go. And so, ever so gently, she moved on.

She was attracted to Claude by his name. Not only because it was the mirror image of her own but because it implied Gallic origins, and there are few things more exotic in the eyes of a girl of tender years than a Continental. No matter how many times Claude insisted that he was born in Beaconsfield to a mother with pretensions, who named her daughter Madeleine (after Proust, *naturellement*) and that he'd never so much as set foot in France, Claudia would have none of it. In order to humour her therefore Claude adopted a French accent, which seemed to do the trick, so long as he remembered. He was happy enough to go along with this, to whisper sweet *riens* into Claudia's ears – it was the French after all who first invented *l'amour* – and stroll side by side with her through the orchard of the family home under an August moon. He was even allowed to hold Claudia's hand, and kiss her softly on the cheek. Beyond this however Claudia drew the line. When Claude attempted to do what every Frenchman, real or fake, has always wanted to do with a young woman since the beginnings of time, she pulled back, and continued to pull back until, out of patience, he left in search of other distractions.

So far, so frustrating. Love seemed to elude Claudia, so that at the age of sixteen she assumed she was incapable of it and should resign herself to remaining an old maid for the rest of her life. In the meantime however she set her sights on the immensely tall Ambrose Holmondesley. Once again it was the name that attracted her, as the correct pronunciation of it bore absolutely no resemblance to the way it was spelt, thus separating the ones in the know, who pronounced it 'Humsley', to the ones who claimed an acquaintance they did not have, who took it at face value. All of which tickled Claudia pink.

'Hums' as he became known, was so intensely aristocratic he was able to speak without seeming to open his mouth, and he was supremely gracious to everyone equally. He had a curious way of leaning forwards at a slight diagonal when talking to Claudia, as if she were the only person in the entire world, which she naturally found enchanting. But when she watched him do the exact same thing in conversation with the gardener she was disappointed. The only person in the entire world after all must be the only person in the entire world. Besides, Claudia had a sneaking suspicion that Hums was not what one might call a lady's man. Or a man's man come to that. Or rather, that he was both, yet neither. In other words, that he was not interested in women *as such*.

It was all beginning to look rather hopeless. Yet Claudia was determined to have one last go.

Her Prince Charming this time was a genial soul called Bertram. He was neither fearsomely aristocratic nor exotically French nor endearingly clumsy. His *modus operandi*, if one can use such a phrase, was humour. He was an accomplished *raconteur* and teller of tall tales, which is a gift many young men would give their right arm for. To be able to make a person, especially a female person, laugh is a skill that attracts attention and adoration all over the world. Thus Claudia, who had the ability to laugh at a story she had heard told several times over, decided she had found her soul mate.

So for some time it was 'Bertie and Claudie', and while they sounded like a circus act they were the most popular pair in the set in which they moved. They were known as Beauty and the Bard, which was only slightly misleading because Bertie was perfectly capable of breaking into a form of doggerel if asked to. He was, in addition to being an inexhaustible comedian, a very *accommodating* sort of person, in public at least.

So what went wrong here?

Anyone who has known anyone who makes a living by making people laugh, from Shakespeare's Feste to the famous clown Grimaldi, realises that at heart they are melancholy people. Why exhaust yourself making jokes at home when you spend all your waking hours doing so in public? It's what we would now call a busman's holiday.

The same applied to Bertie. On the relatively rare occasions when he and Claudia were alone together he sank into a morass of moroseness. She could get not so much as peep out of him. She did her best to engage him in conversation, switching topics every other minute in an attempt to get him to join in; but all he could manage was the odd grunt, and a wave of a hand as if to say 'Leave me alone, I'm exhausted'. He was like one of those little puppet figures on a chiming clock, who appear from apertures on the hour to dance like a dervish while the clock is striking before retreating back into the darkness for the next 59 minutes. Out of the limelight, in the dark, Bertie was inert.

On this occasion however this was not enough to deter Claudia. Having learned that setting out to change people did not work, she tried another tack: she attempted to become like him. She learned to be morose, to read, and occasionally to quote, miserable poetry about suicidal poets in dreary garrets. Not only did that not work, it sent Bertram into a fury. He accused her of mocking him, of making fun of the precious, misunderstood state of manic depression which, he seemed to imply, he had a monopoly on.

And the sad thing was – or was it sad, or was it what after all Claudia was looking for? – this time for some reason she found it difficult to move on. It was as if there were an invisible thread joining her to this sad/happy-faced clown, this complex piece of humanity the like of which she had never met before. The more her friends tried to shake sense into her the more she remonstrated, through her tears, that this was 'the one'.

Her heart, in a phrase, was truly broken. Or perhaps that should be 'broken in'. Like a wild pony she had been tamed, and suppressed. She had achieved her rite of passage, she had come up against the kind of love that shreds your heartstrings and leaves you gasping for breath, and she didn't like it much.

So by the time she reached seventeen years old Claudia was considerably more confused about love than she'd been a year before. Having learned you should never set out to change a man as you'll dislike him if you don't succeed and dislike him even more if you do; that men who pass themselves off as French when they are not are not to be trusted (she had a confused memory); and that the one thing worse than trying to change a man is trying to change yourself in order to appeal to a man, she'd also absorbed the most fundamental lesson of all: that a girl should never show her true feelings to a man as she will leave him nothing to strive for. The art of love, in short, required practice, judgement and above all, deviousness.

You would think after all that most women would have said – Enough. There are other, simpler ways of passing one's time, other occupations far more pleasurable, with predictable outcomes, that don't wreck your appetite and threaten your self-esteem. Why spend your time and your energy on the pursuit of something so unpredictable, so all-consuming, so ultimately *ludicrous* as attempting to fall in love?

You might as well have sung to the birds in the trees.

Mother love

I realised something was wrong the day my mother stopped nagging me.

Punctuality had always been important to her, but once it started not to matter, when she was living in sheltered housing and there were few deadlines or appointments and nothing had to be done by any particular time, it became an obsession. If I was ten minutes late from driving across London to see her I knew to expect several minutes of dressing-down before we could begin a conversation.

By then our relationship had become mostly utilitarian. We discussed bills and payments, shopping and pension issues and that was about it. That at least was safe. Anything else was, and had always been, dangerous.

To cite an example:

'Do your friends use table napkins?'

It was some years ago. We had gone abroad together to attend my brother's wedding and we were sharing the same hotel room.

By way of explanation, short of scrolling through forty years of our mother-daughter relationship: suffice to say my mother was not interested in table napkins so much as the sort of people I was mixing with and whether or not they used table napkins; and if they did, whether they were paper ones – which was acceptable, cotton or linen creating unnecessary laundry – or whether they eschewed napkins altogether, or worse, used kitchen paper, either of which rendered them in her eyes socially beyond the pale. There being so satisfactory answer to her heavily loaded question therefore I believe I mumbled something like 'I don't know', at which she announced that since I seemed incapable of conducting an ordinary conversation she would never speak to me again.

That was how it was.

~

As years went by it got better and it also got worse. The more my mother found herself having to depend on me for the smallest thing the more difficult she became. The mother-daughter baggage that had always lurked in the corner of the room began to fill up more and more space. There was a lot of biting of tongues and occasionally, not often enough, an apology, usually coming first from her and then from me – *No it was my fault, I shouldn't have said/done/questioned* . . . It turned into a ridiculous, childish dance and neither of us seemed able or willing to stop it.

Then one day the nagging stopped, quite suddenly, overnight actually. For a tiny moment I thought my mother had had a kind of brainstorm, or perhaps that she'd come to her senses after all these years. But then I saw the faraway look on her face and I realised she had at last gone to a place where nobody, myself included, could reach her. After a month or two of this and several trips to the doctor I – and he – came to the conclusion it was neither a blip nor a brainstorm. It was set in. And so I did that dreadful thing, I put my mother into a home.

'*I put my mother into a home*'. How easy it sounds.

It is not just the deed that makes all daughters, and a few sons as well, cringe with guilt. It is the unilateral acknowledgment of the handing over of power. I am now making my mother's decisions, whether she likes it or not, and she has no say in the matter. Paradoxically this did not make those decisions easier to make, quite the reverse.

In the event however it was all comparatively easy, because for the first time in her life my mother, my hitherto demanding yet fiercely independent mother, had become pliant. So there was no fuss and no resistance and, worst of all perhaps, no real comprehension.

It didn't stop me crying of course. But she never did. Or if she did I never saw it.

~

Barbara entered the home at more or less the same time as mum, which is possibly one of the reasons she latched onto her. In the living room, at mealtimes, watching television or drinking tea, they sat together all the time. I'm not quite sure what made Barbara – older but a lot more voluble – seek out my now placid mother, though at the time I did wonder rather cattily if it was because she could talk away at her *ad infinitum* knowing she would not answer back. But I was wrong.

After a month in the home my mother began to speak again, not quite in the way she used to, but fluently and coherently, especially when she was in the company of her new friend.

The conversation was more or less the same.

'Eve and I are old friends, aren't we dear?' Barbara would begin.

'Oh yes,' my mother would reply.

'We met a very long time ago. When we were – where were we?'

'Was it the bridge club?' (My mother never played bridge in her life.)

'Do you know I can't really remember. Or was it at Anthony's house?'

'Anthony? Who's Anthony?'

'Oh Eve, come on! Anthony, you can't have forgotten him.'

'You don't mean Eric, do you?'

'Eric? My son . . .' Barbara would turn quite suddenly to address me directly, 'comes to visit me every day. And he has such a long journey.'

'Does he? That's very good of him,' I'd reply. 'Where does he have to travel from?'

'He lives in Acton.'

'In Acton? But we're in Acton.'

'Eastbourne dear. We're in Eastbourne. Can't you hear the sea?'

'Eastbourne? How lovely.' Humouring two old ladies, who once had brains as sharp as tacks, tacks still sharp but now slightly skewed, made me feel rather sad.

'I always wanted to live in Eastbourne.' And Barbara would lean back in her chair and gaze out of the window, where instead of the little west London garden, with its gazebo and tidy flowerbed, she presumably saw the English Channel crashing against the supports of Eastbourne Pier.

~

From time to time one of them, usually Eve, my mother, would have to go into hospital for a spell and the one remaining, usually Barbara, would retreat to her room. When she did appear, for meals, she would sit and eat in glum silence in her friend's absence, refusing to speak to anyone. And when the absentee returned it was as if she'd never gone, and the conversation continued on without a break.

'My son's on holiday,' Barbara would tell her friend, and it was absolutely true. 'So he won't be visiting for a while. How's your daughter?'

Barbara liked me because I was Eve's daughter. She liked to chat to me about Eve, and their friendship, which went back goodness knows how long, she'd stopped counting the years. She told me about the walks they took along the seafront, but only when it wasn't raining. The sea breeze was so refreshing, and afterwards all she wanted to do was sleep, which she would not allow herself to do because when you get to a certain age and you start taking naps in the afternoon – well, who knows when the nap will end?

Barbara had been a history teacher in her younger days and still retained most of what she had taught. She could recite the Kings and Queens of England without hesitation, though the dates had become a bit hazy now. The best of them in Barbara's view was Edward the Third, she couldn't understand why Shakespeare had ignored him.

Their favourite game, Barbara's and Eve's, which they played virtually every day and which varied little, was 'Guess who's coming to dinner?'. Barbara would list her ideal dinner guests and Eve would chip in, and sometimes they'd have disagreements and get quite argumentative.

'Queen Victoria?' scoffed Barbara. 'Why on earth would you want her? She was dull before she married and even duller when she was widowed and far too busy in between producing all those children. And she was a terrible mother. I don't suppose . . .' this said leaning forwards and muttering into my ear, 'any of *her* offspring would have come all this way to visit their aged mother in a home.' After which she would chuckle for several minutes.

'And who closed down all the theatres?' my mother would scoff back. (She always loved her theatre.) 'How can you possibly have that awful man at your dinner table?'

'Because I would ask him – Mr Cromwell, I would say – what harm is there in fun? How did you get to be such a killjoy? I would get it from the horse's mouth you see.'

'I suppose so,' said Eve, and after a moment's sulky silence, she'd say, 'Well in that case we'd better invite Richard the Third, if you want to get the true story.'

'Oh what a splendid idea! But better not tell him what Shakespeare said about him, he'd be absolutely livid.'

It was all quite logical, and fun, and totally coherent. And I had to come to the rather dismal conclusion that there was nothing really wrong with my mother – it was the company she kept. No one, myself included, had really bothered to talk to her, not properly, until now.

I was pleased, of course, and relieved. And ever so slightly jealous.

~

Eve went into hospital for the last time in December. While she was away Barbara retreated to her room, as usual, and spoke to no one except to ask where her friend was, which she did several times a day.

When my mother died I thought I should break the news to Barbara myself. The carers at the home advised me against it, they said she wouldn't take it in anyway and would be asking after her again the following day and they'd have to break it to her all over again. All the same, I said, she has to be told, she's not a child.

She was in her room, alone. Her face fell momentarily when she saw me, and then lifted again. I was not Eve, but I was the next best person to Eve.

I sat down next to her on her bed.

'I'm afraid Eve died last night, Barbara,' I told her.

There was a very long pause. Barbara was looking down at her hands.

'Was it peaceful?' she asked eventually.

'Yes. A heart attack. She'd had them before if you remember.'

Without looking at me Barbara placed a hand over

mine.

'My dear I am so terribly sorry.'

'Thank you. I'm sorry too, for you.'

'Will there be a funeral?'

'A small one, yes.'

'I won't attend. You don't mind, do you, it's not from disrespect.'

'I totally understand.'

'She was a wonderful woman, your mother,' Barbara went on. 'Throughout her life. She had a lot to put up with, with her first husband especially. He was so cruel.'

'Her first husband?'

'But her second husband, your father, that was a good marriage, don't you think?'

'In a way. Except it wasn't her . . .'

'I think sometimes we have to endure the hardships before we can appreciate the good times, don't you agree?'

'I do.'

'It's what gives a person compassion, which is the greatest of all the virtues, wouldn't you say? Your mother was a very kind woman. It was kindness that made her who she was.'

What could I possibly say to that?

'And she wasn't always that way. Your mother was a very special person Joanna, I will never ever forget her.'

It was the first time she had actually used my name.

She'd kept hold of my hand all this time, and now she squeezed it. And I began to cry. I was crying for my poor uncompassionate mother, who had married only once and then to someone who only loved her in a vague, detached way; who never really experienced hardship but never really got what she needed either, which was passion and engagement.

I was crying because the only person who did give her what she needed was this strange old woman who was sitting here next to me, holding my hand for all the world as if I were her own daughter. Who had only known my mother a few months but managed to convince both Eve and herself that they'd known and loved one another all their lives. Who loved my mother more, truth be known, than I loved her myself.

I was crying because I was grateful, and because whatever love I failed to feel for my mother I felt, right at that particular moment, for Barbara.

The streets of London

It was a chill January morning and Jessica Fitzroy decided to go looking for love. No, not that kind of love, she was not that kind of girl. But she'd been feeling a bit down lately and her friends all seemed to be busy. They led fuller lives than she did, with absorbing jobs, and children, and interesting hobbies. Some of them even had husbands. So on this dreary Sunday soon after Christmas there was no one to play with, and if she stayed inside her four walls she feared she might slip into a kind of depression.

She headed for Piccadilly Circus, for no other reason except that it was in the heart of London, and of course it was home to Eros, god of love. Perched on the ball of one foot on a plinth, having just shot his arrow in the direction of . . . well, there's a thing: the number of times she's been to Piccadilly Circus but could she think which direction the statue was facing?

She emerged from the station and looked for the naked god. He was facing towards Lower Regent Street, the arrow aimed slightly downwards, and she had a bizarre thought that if she were to place herself right in the line of fire, what might happen then? She had to jostle for position somewhat, she was not the only one trying to take a photo from that point. She bristled slightly at the thought that she could be mistaken for a tourist in the town she'd lived in all her life.

From there she headed up Shaftesbury Avenue, named after the Earl of Shaftesbury, the famous philanthropist who did so much for the poor in Victorian times, despite – or maybe because of – having been brought up by aristocratic parents who took very little notice of him. What was it about the upper-class, Jessica mused, that they found it so hard to love their own children? And how interesting that this particular neglected child went on to dedicate his adult life to helping the downtrodden and the unloved, particularly the children. Was he a loving father, she wondered? Or did he, like other well-known philanthropists such as Charles Dickens, find it easier to love the public in general than his own family?

With this thought in mind Jessica decided to make a quick detour away from Shaftesbury Avenue to St Anne's churchyard to pay tribute to the grave of the once renowned and now almost forgotten figure of William Hazlitt.

Jessica had studied English literature at university, a decision she often regretted as in her view a concentrated study of literature is a sure way of killing one's enjoyment of it. But she would always be grateful for having been introduced to Hazlitt, the essayist, critic, writer and painter – was there anything these bygone characters *couldn't* do? – and in particular to his remarkable confessional piece *Liber Amoris*.

Hazlitt, who was married at the time, fell in love at first sight with his landlord's daughter Sarah, despite the fact she was seventeen and half his age. He worshipped her, with the kind of all-consuming adoration that shuts out the rest of the world and plays havoc with a man's reason. Sarah aided and abetted, up to a point, by spending whole evenings with Hazlitt in his room, perched upon his knee, kissing and cuddling. Yet despite her shows of affection she resisted Hazlitt's marriage proposals, and in time he began to have suspicions about her. When one day he came across her strolling down the street arm in arm with another man, his life imploded. And such is the nature of these things, the love that had dominated his life for three years or more turned in an instant to hate, and then to intense jealousy.

Hazlitt then went on to commit what was considered professional suicide in those days by writing about the affair, in open and graphic detail, in a book called *Liber Amoris*. His friends were horrified. His colleagues were disgusted. It took years before he was able to re-establish himself and his reputation.

What puzzled Jessica about all this was: if love is the unity of hearts and minds, then how could a man like Hazlitt, who was one of the sharpest-brained, original- and broad-thinking men of his time, who loved nothing better than to spend hours with friends and acquaintances discussing everything from art to politics to philosophy to theatre, throw his life away on a girl who showed not a flicker of interest in any of those things? What did they find to talk about during those evenings spent with Sarah on his knee? There must have been a limit to the sweet nothings, even for a man like Hazlitt.

There was no logical answer to the question, of course. And while all this may have done nothing for Hazlitt's reputation in his own time it did the opposite for Jessica three centuries later. There was something uniquely endearing about a clever man who allows himself to be led so openly and completely by his emotions, even if they did lead him into a dark place. It was infinitely preferable to those high-flown writers who wrote about love without ever having experienced it.

As she stood looking down at the modest grave in the corner of what she thought was a deserted graveyard, yards from the bustle of Shaftesbury Avenue, Jessica was aware of a figure appearing at her side.

'I was just looking at all the names,' said the stranger. 'And you wouldn't believe there's a Mark and a Charles and a Rachel, just like in my family, and you couldn't spare 99p for a burger could you?'

Jessica was afraid of beggars. They spooked her, she found it difficult to look them in the eye, they could be her, or she them. But today was going to be different. Today she was going to give to everyone, even try to talk to them. No matter the woman who stood right by her looked relatively well turned-out, and cheerful, and her breath smelled of alcohol. Jessica opened her purse and popped a pound coin in the woman's hand, and with a smile and a thanks she was gone.

Jessica left the churchyard and made her way along Shaftesbury Avenue towards Chinatown.

She hated London, at times. Most of the time. It had not brought her the fame and status she had dreamed of as a young thing. Nor had her personal life made up for professional disappointment. A childless marriage that had lasted barely five years. Several lovers and boyfriends, of various degrees of unsuitability, as she believed that anyone who could genuinely love her must be deficient in some way. And this city. This over-crowded, drab, frantic city where everyone was in a hurry and no one connected.

She was in Covent Garden now, where Eliza first bumped into Professor Higgins, that pompous, childish misogynist created by Bernard Shaw. How disappointing that when they turned it into a musical they felt they had to change the ending; so instead of Eliza deserting Higgins to run off with the adoring Freddie to start up a flower shop, as Shaw had her do, she came skulking back to spend the rest of her life with the man who had treated her like a talking doll. When it came to women Shaw was ahead of his time, and definitely ahead of Lerner and Loewe half a century years later.

True love. Maybe true love, love without conflict, is too boring to be written about, thought Jessica.

There were no beggars in Covent Garden. They would have been upstaged by the mime artists, the Yodas, frozen as statues, and the street entertainers. This being a Sunday, albeit in the middle of winter, Covent Garden was seething, and not only with tourists but with families with kids, enjoying the free entertainment. The joy on a child's face is a thing to behold, thought Jessica. The joy that is in the moment, that's not concerned with having to be somewhere or doing something else, that can stand stock still on the plaza at Covent Garden and become completely absorbed in the antics of a fire-eater or a juggler or whatever exotic performer this crazy city has to offer.

This crazy city. She loved it too, at times, but only because she was used to it.

Corin. Now why should Corin suddenly enter her consciousness?

Corin had been a busker once. He fancied himself as a musician, he played the squeezebox, not particularly well, but he had such a sunny personality he managed to make a fair whack outside Green Park tube station in the morning rush-hour.

Corin was one of the nicest people she'd ever met. He had not an unkind word to say of anyone, least of all Jessica. She wondered at times if he might not have been just a bit simple. He encouraged her with her art, he tried to get her to tour the galleries with her portfolio, he even suggested she hire her own space and hold her own one-person exhibition. He made it sound so easy, as people do who don't understand the business. He infuriated her. But he was one of the kindest of people. She wondered what happened to him.

She was in the Strand now. The Savoy, where her parents once took her to a tea dance. A tea dance! Impossible to imagine it now. The waiters were *so* polite, she thought for a moment they were taking the piss, as she was after all only a child then. And a disappointment to her glamorous mother. 'Oh do sit up straight Jessica, and why do you have to wear that awful *cardigan?*'

She felt comfortable in cardigans. They made a person invisible.

On she went, along one of those narrow little streets that lead down to the embankment, where the rain, which had been hum-ing and hah-ing for some time now, suddenly made up its mind and started chucking it down. She was on the verge of packing it in, yet she forced herself to keep on going towards the river.

She was fond of the Thames. It had dignity, as if it had been there for ever, which it had, and had seen everything, which it also had. Even though there could not have been a drop of water in it that was more than – what – a few weeks old, maybe a month? Who knew? There was still ancient treasure lurking in those drops – Roman coins, the odd Bronze Age axe, Tudor pottery – foraged by archaeologists and mudlarks several thousand years after they had been discarded. It was one of many reasons the river deserved one's respect.

Old Father Thames had been a fixture ever since the Romans made camp at Southwark two thousand years ago. It had seen ship-building and ship-breaking, ships heading for war against the Spanish Armada or the French or the Germans. Ships carrying and delivering textiles and spices to and from the furthest reaches of the globe. Boats ferrying commuters from home on the north side to work on the south, and back again. Imagine the bustle and the business.

Two hundred years ago it was known as the Great Stink, on account of what had been deposited into it. It was an open sewer running through the heart of the city. And now, so they say, it is cleaner than it has ever been and even harbours the odd seal.

Wordsworth immortalised the Thames on Westminster Bridge – now *there* was a romantic if ever there was one.

> *'Earth has not anything to show more fair:*
> *Dull would he be of soul who could pass by*
> *A sight so touching in its majesty. . .'*

Astonishing how the words stuck.

> *' . . . Ne'er saw I, never felt, a calm so deep!*
> *The river glideth at his own sweet will:*
> *Dear God! the very houses seem asleep;*
> *And all that mighty heart is lying still!'*

It could bring the tears to your eyes. What a man Wordsworth must have been, to have seen so much beauty in that heaving mass of grey, stinking slurry. Because slurry it would have been then, back in 1800 or whenever it was.

Standing now on Waterloo Bridge, even in the belting rain and with the January wind whipping Jessica's cheeks, there was a view to behold. St Paul's, the Walkie-Talkie and the Cheesegrater. The London Eye and the National Theatre. And around the bend of the river and just out of sight, the Tower of London. The old and the new huddled together, celebrating the two thousand odd years of London's existence. It was enough to make a person feel almost proud.

As she reached the halfway point on the bridge the rain that had been coming down in sheets suddenly let up, as if someone had flipped a switch, and in an instant the sky was lit with a weird golden glow that was quite unreal. And there, reaching across the water from the unprepossessing hulk of the National Theatre to the grey expanse of Somerset House, was a rainbow.

Jessica took a photo. She took several. She would paint it, as soon as she got home. And not just the rainbow but that beautiful, unearthly golden light behind the dark silhouette of the Houses of Parliament behind her. Then even before the thought had vanished from her mind she dismissed it. She knew she could not do it justice.

There. That was the crux of it. She was, in the end, a mediocre painter. She had never been anything else. She was an excellent picture researcher – that was easy, it was the kind of finite job that once you got the hang of it, you could do it with your eyes closed. And where's the satisfaction in a job you know you can do?

That reminded her of the story of Bernard Shaw's friend, an engineer as she remembered, one of the best in the business, who wanted above all to be a playwright. He hounded Shaw with script after script, which the playwright read with increasing irritation, because, frankly, his friend could not write to save his life, and he told him so. But his friend persisted. Shaw could not understand why a man who was known and revered throughout the world as a genius in his field insisted on putting all his energies into something at which he was at best mediocre. Jessica understood completely.

And that story, perversely perhaps, along with the sudden change in the weather, made Jessica feel a whole lot better.

As she approached the concrete jungle that is the South Bank it seemed the change in the weather had brought out a whole new crowd of people. They were Sunday people, in no hurry, going nowhere in particular, for no particular purpose. People with *time.* Strolling, most of them. Elderly couples holding hands.

She walked on past the concrete bunker of the National Theatre and downriver to Gabriel's Wharf. She was reminded of one morning years ago when she'd stood there on the embankment, with Tim, at low tide, looking down onto the foreshore where sculptors were carving mermaids out of the wet sand. She had marvelled at the effort they put into creating something that would only last a couple of hours before the Thames tide washed it away, and Tim had pronounced, in his obscure way, that all this industry for something so fleeting was a metaphor for our lives. She had no idea what he was talking about at the time, but it had come to that stage in their marriage when she could no longer be bothered to ask him.

What children they were.

Beyond Gabriel's Wharf she came upon a woman sitting on the ground with her back to the river, head bent into her lap as if in prayer, outstretched hands clutching a polystyrene cup. Her submissiveness made Jessica feel both tearful and irritated. She dropped a coin into the cup and the scarved woman looked up briefly and gave her a wan smile before resuming her prayer position. She could be a total fraud, Jessica thought. But nothing on God's good earth would have me sitting on a wet, cold concrete walkway in the fading light of this winter's day. She would have liked to have struck up some kind of a conversation but the woman's attitude did not invite it, so instead Jessica reached out and touched her fleetingly on the arm. It broke her heart to think of people who were forced to leave their own country, for whatever reason, to make a home in a place like London. It distressed her to think anyone should have to leave a place to which they felt they belonged.

In the tunnel under Blackfriars Bridge the man playing

the accordion badly did not even acknowledge Jessica's contribution. Never mind. You can't buy love with a coin in a busker's cap.

What happened with Corin? Did she leave him or did he leave her? She had herself down as the one who is always left. But on reflection she acknowledged she may have laid the groundwork for the leaving; like the grumpy employee who hates her job and makes it obvious but refuses to quit until pushed. In the case of Jessica's marriage it was a younger model that did it for them in the end; but it was Jessica who had created the vacuum into which the younger model had, understandably, taken up position. In the end, she only had herself to blame for most of what had happened in her life.

The light was dwindling now. That was another irritant. Four o'clock in the afternoon and already it was beginning to get dark. The golden glow behind Westminster had dimmed to a muddy grey.

The long long nights of an English winter were hard to cope with, even if you did have a warm place to go home to. She wondered if the humble supplicant in the scarf had such a home, or the burger-eating lady in the graveyard. She thought they probably did. She did hope so.

Just then something unexpected gave a lift to Jessica's spirits. As the daylight went so the bridges of the City of London began to light up – colours of purple, red, green and yellow, changing before your eyes, operated by some invisible computer to react to movement, bringing the city to life again.

There was love around. It wasn't always visible, or tangible. It was there in the sometimes trivial, sometimes monumental generosity of individuals, past and present. The Earl of Shaftesburys and the Thomas Corams of centuries past, who established schools for the destitute and the Foundling Hospital for orphaned children. The

American actor Sam Wanamaker, who conceived the idea of building a brand new replica Globe Theatre on the banks of the Thames in honour of William Shakespeare. The unknown artists who lit up the City bridges. London wasn't just a city of money, trade and imperial exploitation. It was a hub of art and history, philanthropy and global culture and humanity. It may be grubby, crowded and worn at the edges. But most importantly, to Jessica, it was home.

She stood there for some time, gazing across the water to St Paul's. She would go home soon. And she would paint that scene of the light behind Parliament, to the best of her ability. She would create her finest mermaid.

And then she'd look up Corin McNally on Facebook.

The Good Samaritan

Alice worked at the ticket desk of a small museum off Chancery Lane. It was a niche museum that held the private collection of a gentleman by the name of Anton de Courcey, maintained by private bequest and comprising an eclectic mishmash of weird and wonderful paintings, artefacts, sculptures and furniture from all over the world. It didn't get a lot of visitors, which is how they liked it. They didn't need the money and they knew, and Alice in particular knew, that the people who did venture through the door were rather special people, as it was not on the usual tourist trail and so far had not received any particular mention on social media or sites such as Tripadvisor.

The job suited Alice down to the ground. She was fascinated by people and she liked to get into conversation with them as they came through the door. She would begin with 'How did you hear about us?' and take it from there. Many of the visitors were elderly and most of them arrived in pairs – husband and wife, or two friends, usually women. But now and again there would be a single visitor and it was she – usually it was a she – who interested Alice in particular; as in why would anyone want to visit a museum on their own? She was not passing judgment, far from it, she was simply curious, and the assumption had to be it was because they could not find anyone to go with them.

Alice understood loneliness. It was the scourge of modern life, so it was said, with so many people living on their own now, elderly people in particular, although loneliness was not confined to the elderly, far from it. What with online shopping and the internet in general it was all too easy to go for days without speaking to anyone. Which was terrifically sad in Alice's opinion as human beings were gregarious animals in her view and she knew all too well how scary the world could be, and how easy and tempting it was to withdraw from it.

She would latch on to these single visitors, given half a chance. She'd offer to guide them around the museum, give them a personal tour if you like, so long as the manager Richard was around to take her place at the ticket desk for a spell. She loved doing this. She knew everything there was to know about every exhibit, she'd made a point of it, and it gave her a particular thrill to be able to share this knowledge with a complete stranger. Knowing she could lighten up their lives for just a moment or two gave her more pleasure than anyone could imagine.

One day she decided to take this a step further. There was this young woman, in her thirties maybe, quite attractive, on her own. When Alice asked her the usual question on her arrival she shrugged and said something about passing by and seeing the sign on the door, and . . . she shrugged again. So Alice took this to mean the woman was on her own and looking for something to do and somewhere to go, which she found rather sad. She was not able to give the woman her personal conducted tour – Richard not being in evidence – but as the lonely visitor was on her way out Alice asked her where she was going next. It was a cheeky question but one she thought she could get away with because she accompanied it with a broad smile, so the woman could be reassured she was just being friendly and unthreatening.

On this occasion however the woman stared at Alice so mournfully it broke her heart, and once again she shrugged and muttered something like 'I've no idea' – or that's what Alice thought she said. It so happened at that precise moment that Richard arrived from outside, rather out of breath, and to everyone's surprise, including Alice's, she found herself saying to the young stranger, 'Shall we find somewhere nearby to have a coffee?'

It startled the young woman, needless to say, so Alice took advantage of her surprise by grabbing her coat and with a nod to Richard and a 'back soon' she edged the stranger out of the door until they were standing side by side on the street. She knew the exact place of course, around the corner, so she grabbed the woman's arm and virtually marched her there. The woman didn't protest. She didn't say or do anything in fact, which confirmed in Alice's mind the fact that she was a lonely soul who quite possibly didn't live in London, or she didn't know her way around, and what she could do with was a friendly chat with someone she didn't know.

Alice sat her down and asked her what she wanted and she said herbal tea, so she went to the counter and ordered two herbal teas – it was not Alice's usual tipple but she did it to be friendly. The woman did not offer to pay for it and nor did Alice ask or expect her to.

She established the woman's name was Marta, but beyond that she was not forthcoming. She still seemed a bit startled by the whole business and it occurred to Alice that perhaps she thought she was trying to pick her up, in some bizarre fashion – imagine that! So instead, and by way of encouragement, Alice told Marta about herself. How she was born and bred in London, in Putney, where she went to school, how she'd studied history at university and how she got to work at the museum. It was her first proper job, she'd never quite managed to hold jobs down before – for some reason what she had thought were long-term contracts turned out not to be. This one came about because a distant friend of Alice's knew one of the trustees of the museum, and they said they were looking for someone friendly and reliable who wasn't about to go off and get pregnant – perish the thought! She'd been there nearly a year now and she absolutely loved it. She loved the feeling of the place, the intimacy, the quirkiness of the exhibits, and most of all she loved meeting the visitors, they were so interesting, and unusual.

Through all of this Marta did not say a word. Not one. It occurred to Alice at one point that perhaps she didn't understand English, as she did not react to anything Alice said, though she was looking at her throughout, always with that blank expression. So in the end even Alice was compelled to admit defeat. It was she who made the first move – 'Well, guess I'd better be getting back' – and they parted company on the pavement outside the coffee shop; and it may have looked to the random passer-by that Marta waited to see which way Alice went before she headed off in the opposite direction.

Ah well, you can't win them all, so Alice realised. On that occasion she'd misread things, it happens.

The next opportunity was more successful however.

He was an elderly man, not too steady on his feet, so Alice whipped out the folding wheelchair they kept in the cloakroom for just this sort of occasion and offered him her private tour of the exhibits. She went so far as to close the door to the museum while she did so, Richard not being present.

He was chatty, said his name was Miklos and he was an émigré from Hungary and had lived in London for the whole of his adult life. He had no children and had lost his wife two years ago.

He ticked all Alice's boxes perfectly. Moreover he seemed interested to know about her, in a harmlessly avuncular way – where she lived (Stoke Newington), did she have brothers or sisters (one brother she never saw), where were her parents (both dead), what were her aspirations (none in particular). They passed a very pleasant forty-five minutes together and he was genuinely appreciative of her time and her knowledge. Had she had half a chance she would have whipped him around the corner to her favourite coffee house for further chats, but Richard's absence, plus a slight feeling of guilt at having closed up shop for forty-five minutes meant she had to see him to the front door and wave goodbye from the pavement outside. He was as ever wobbly on his feet, but she watched and marvelled as, like so many elderly people who simply assume the traffic will stop as they cross the road, he just launched himself into the middle of it. Unfortunately at that moment there came hurtling around the corner a blue van, the driver of which had not apparently read the rule book, and in order to avoid hitting the aged pedestrian standing right in his path he swerved violently and careered onto the pavement, colliding instead with the young woman standing there with her mouth open.

~

It was a couple of weeks before Alice regained anything approaching full consciousness. She had several broken bones in her right leg and some internal damage, fortunately neither life-threatening nor –changing. She was still pretty well out of it when the first visitors began arriving so she didn't immediately recognise them. The one she did immediately recognise was Miklos. He'd been coming almost every day since the accident, so the nurses told her, which he claimed was entirely his fault, and if anything happened to this sweet young lady – as he put it – he could never forgive himself. They asked him if he was a relative and he said he was *in loco* in a sense since she didn't have any surviving family members. His face when Alice first opened her eyes was a picture of joy and relief, though she wasn't yet able to focus sufficiently to see it properly. They told her later, the nurses, that he had held onto her hand all the time he was there and had to be forcibly removed from her bedside when they needed to attend to her.

There were other visitors too whom she could not place, though after a moment she recognised the image of the tall man with light brown hair and the ginger beard as her brother. His face was such a picture of anxiety it made her laugh. He too held her hand and said as soon as she was well enough to leave hospital she was to come and convalesce with him and his wife at their home in Suffolk.

There were friends from school whom she thought she'd lost touch with, and others who claimed to have worked with her in her past jobs. Richard was there too, as was a young woman with dark hair whom she couldn't place.

It seems that Richard had gone to some considerable trouble to hunt down past visitors to the museum who had signed the visitors' book with an especial mention of Alice, which were many. Not all of them were traceable, naturally, but those that were were appalled to hear of the accident and some of them made a point of travelling right across town to visit her. These acts of extraordinary kindness touched Alice so deeply she cried.

The dark-haired woman, she eventually remembered, was Marta, her silent friend. She was still silent, but she looked at Alice with such compassion, she even held her hand briefly and stroked it, and Alice could swear she saw a tear in the corner of the woman's eye.

Alice asked Richard about her job, whether or not he would keep it open for her. He looked at her for a long moment before he nodded and said, 'Do you understand now how loved you are?'

She stared at him with incomprehension.

'You thought you were doing people a favour, I could see that,' he was sitting on a chair next to her and he'd placed his elbows on the bed. 'You got it into your head the whole world out there was just waiting for your friendly smile, a word from you to fill the empty void of their lives. Not everyone is lonely. Not even you.'

'Not even me.' Alice lent back into the pillows and closed her eyes. 'Not even me.'

21st century woman (part 1)

This three-part poem was a song I wrote for a musical called 'IT'
in 2000. I was rather proud of having written an entire song
with virtually no rhyming lyrics.

MEETING

It was a perfectly ordinary day,
I was somewhere in central London,
Doing nothing in particular,
Not feeling special in any way.
Then I looked up and I saw him,
Caught his eye – didn't really mean to,
And from that moment on
I was drowning.

My organs were turning to jelly,
And my heart was hamm'ring so loudly,
I could feel the pavement vibrating,
On that far from ordinary day.
And he smiled, though he had no right to,
And he walked right up and he spoke to me:
'Have you got the time?' he said.

Fourteen years at school,
Three at university,
Years of climbing the corporate ladder
To get where I am today.
Here on a London pavement
Stammering 'It's coming up to a qu-qu-quarter to ten.
Please don't go, don't go - please stay
For the rest of my life.'
(I didn't say that last bit, naturally.)

I'm a 21st century woman,
Pragmatic and single-minded,
Got a career, a suit and a laptop,
I can hold my own in a boardroom.
But I'm afraid you'll have to forgive me,
'Cause I'm not the person I was.
Though equality
Once meant the world to me,
Now it's gone,
Flown
Right out of the window.

I'm a 21st century woman,
Mature and independent,
Got a brain, a degree and ambition,
Always knew where I was going.
But I'm afraid you're going to despise me,
'Cause I'm not the woman I was.
And I know after all,
I am not in control,
You can take all the rest of my life
For this moment.

Tokens of love

She had no recognition of the thing that was growing inside her for all the forty weeks it was there. She joked she was harbouring a plastic toy, the sort of thing you found at the bottom of cornflakes packets, except she wasn't joking, it was what she really felt. She wore Laura Ashley dresses and truly imagined the bump was not visible, long after it was blindingly obvious to the most casual passer-by.

So when she gave birth to a healthy boy with all its fingers and toes intact, and an alertness and eyes that seemed to gaze around and take everything in right from the word go – even though she was told this was not possible – she felt she'd been struck by a thunderbolt. It was a love so overwhelming it blanked out the entire world. Nothing else mattered. Nothing else existed. Wars, famine, global apocalypse, you could have annihilated the world and she would not have noticed, or cared.

The fierceness of the love persisted, through the sleepless nights and despite the anxiety and the exhaustion and the realisation she'd produced the most wilful creature who ever toddled the earth. It persisted, with blips here and there, throughout early school days and the letting go – no more hand holding, no more taking and picking up. Cuddles became fewer, and then non existent, except at Christmas time when there was no one around to see but the immediate family. He was still scribbling kisses on his letters home from university, and when letters became obsolete he would still end his emails with a couple of xx, though they too became fewer as the years passed and they disappeared altogether.

Tokens of love. She kept some of his early stuff from school to remind herself of the loving boy he used to be. They would crop up, the tokens, in unexpected places, such as the lop-sided heart he'd attempted to sculpt in Fimo that she discovered at the bottom of the bin in the kitchen, or the scatter poem he wrote when he was trying to master the typewriter: two lines from a nursery rhyme followed by an expletive, and 'You do love me don't you mum'. The Mother's Day cards he drew at school, with fifteen hearts, each one inside the other, and another one that read: 'There were many times when leaving home seemed the only thing to do. So thank you for staying.'

Through all his young adulthood she did all she could not to burden him with the weight of her love. She waited at least a day before replying to his emails. She phoned him no more than once a week, then once a month. She stepped back and watched as he was posted overseas in some obscure position with the Foreign Office she never quite understood, despite his attempts to explain it to her. She did not complain when he stopped responding to her emails or her calls. 'He's a boy,' her friends would say. She watched as his reputation grew, along with his status, as his pronouncements on international affairs were quoted far and wide. She followed his progress through social media and tried not to respond too often to his tweets.

Love was not a word that cropped up much in her family, but that did not mean it wasn't there. She was, secretly, a touch sceptical about fellow mums who ended phone calls with a chirpy 'Love you!' Say it too often and it doesn't mean anything. She demonstrated her love through her restraint, through her silence, and her absence, through the spare room in her flat that she told him once, and only once, was his if or whenever he needed it, as was she. Just occasionally her self-imposed invisibility made her bristle, and she'd have liked to have told him, but knew she never would, something to the effect of – Do you know how hard it is for me to keep my distance like this, when all I really want to do is wrap you in a bearhug? Do you understand how often I chide myself for feeling upset at your silence? How much I miss those long-afternoon conversations about everything and anything from football to the Greek philosophers, who I'd secretly done a course on so I could try and keep up with you?

But just as she was in danger of sinking into self-pity, along would come a surprise: the 60th birthday party, organised by him single-handedly, over months, in total secret. The unexpected appearance at her 70th, and at her bedside after her cancer operation. Still the word love did not arise, but another word – perhaps more meaningful, and one which made her choke so much she could barely speak: Proud. 'I am proud of you mum'.

That'll do.

A child owes nothing to his creators. He did not ask to come into the world and he did not ask to be loved. A mother's love is rarely reciprocated, it could not, should not be. When his children come along he'll understand. Maybe. Meanwhile it's enough to know that she is twice the woman she was, thanks to him, and thanks also to him she knows beyond all doubt she is capable of that mystical and dangerous thing called unconditional love.

The Turning Point

*'All happy families are alike; each unhappy family is
unhappy in its own way.'*
Tolstoy, *Anna Karenina*.

'Mirrie, come and look at this!' said Keith.

Such an innocuous remark. But to understand its significance, and how it could have marked the turning point of an enduring marriage, it is necessary to explain a few things.

Keith was in the garden. Miranda was working on her computer in the kitchen, which was, and had been since lockdown two months ago, her office.

She was working from home. Keith was furloughed. Which meant they were both at home but their statuses were quite different. While Keith had all the time in the world – which sounds wonderful but isn't necessarily – Miranda felt under extra pressure. After a couple of months it didn't seem that Keith was any more aware of the fact that from 9 to 5pm every day she was not there. She was there in a physical sense, obviously, but in every other sense she was elsewhere. She was working. Her mind was on her work. She could not, would not, drop everything in order to step outside to see what it was that happened to have caught Keith's attention. That he expected her to was typical of him. He was a man. A man moreover who was not sensitive to his surroundings. The sort of man who could walk into a room talking, oblivious of the fact he was interrupting a conversation that was already taking place.

So this seemingly innocuous remark was significant in a number of ways:

It meant, yet again, Keith was unaware of the fact that Miranda was, in fact, not there.

If she did indulge him she would only be encouraging him.

If she did not indulge him she would be wondering, forever more, i) what it was he wanted her to take a look at and ii) whether or not, after all, she cared more about her work than her marriage. Moreover she was doubly furious that she had been thrown into this quandary in the first place, and that her concentration had been ruined anyway, which meant she may as well have indulged him from the start. Except. Except etc. etc. etc.

So Miranda ignored Keith. When he came back in she pretended to be concentrating on her computer screen. He stood in the doorway of the kitchen for a moment, looking at her.

'Did you hear what I said?' he asked.

'Mm?' she said, not looking up.

'Never mind,' said Keith. And he went.

This was not like him. Keith was one of those men who wouldn't recognise a snub if it smacked him in the face, not as a rule. For him to just go, like that, with no further word, with no hint of the magical object that had caught his fascination in the garden, was untypical, and disturbing. Now Miranda's concentration was completely wrecked. Should she go after him and ask him what he was talking about? Apologise? Bearing in mind all the above, she felt she was justified, had been justified. She had ignored him. Short of posting a message on the fridge that said 'Between 9 and 5pm I am not here. Do not try to speak to me.' she didn't know what she could do to get it through his fat skull.

But then what if it the 'this' had been something that, say, moved? Like a bird, or an animal? Or even a feature of the weather – the wind in the trees maybe, a strange cloud – something transient? A now or never sort of thing? Animals and birds don't necessary wait until 5pm to be fascinating.

Miranda sat back in her chair and listened. There was no sound, other than distant traffic. Had he gone out? If so that was, potentially, serious. She sat for some time more, unmoving. She'd been crunching data, which had to be one of the most boring tasks in the world, and now she'd lost her place, and her concentration. There was little point in trying to do any more.

She got up and went out into the garden and looked around. It was a small garden, paved, with a few shrubs and one small apple tree. Not a lot went on in the garden as a general rule. They had a bird-feeder which the squirrels tended to get to first, and there were cats – not theirs, their neighbours – so there weren't many birds around in the first place. Certainly there was nothing that Miranda could see that was remarkable in any way. No rabbits with waistcoats and time-pieces inviting her to adventures underground. Whatever had caught Keith's attention had gone. Flown. Dissolved. If it had been there in the first place.

Keith may never come back. What was there for him to come back for? A grumpy wife, who rarely listened to him, whose head was always buried in her computer? And a job she never enjoyed in the first place, that she never stopped complaining about, but which now seemed to absorb her more than anything else; more than the world around; more than the news; certainly more than her husband. What was going on?

~

Miranda was struggling with lockdown. Paradoxically, with no immediate distraction other than her husband, she found it harder to concentrate on her work, which is why a simple task took her twice as long as it should. This annoyed her. The presence of her husband in the flat, while comforting in some ways – he worked nights, which meant as a general rule they actually got to spend very little time together – was more disrupting than it should have been. Lockdown gave them a once-in-a-lifetime opportunity to do things together, an opportunity they did not take up, mostly because there was nothing to do. Nowhere to go. No pubs, no restaurants, no friends to visit, or to invite home. And now pubs and restaurants were beginning to open up again, and visiting friends was within the guidelines – as far as Miranda could tell, they changed every day, the guidelines, not the friends – they'd somehow got out of the habit of doing things.

Keith meanwhile was coping rather better. He was not one of those people who think every minute of a day should be filled with excitement, or discovery. He did not take up oil painting, or learn a new language. He didn't even work out, or go for long walks, as most men were supposedly doing. He was, in a phrase, content to do very little. And very little was all that was on offer right now.

~

'Mirrie, come and look at this!'

He'd seen the flash of something, in a nearby tree. Something big, and that he'd never seen before. It had swooped down onto the bird-feeder and off again, and now all he could see was a glimpse of something bright green amid the duller green of next door's tree. He kept his eye fixed on it, as if willing it not to go away, to show itself, this bird of paradise, or whatever it was.

There was no reply from Mirrie. He was about to call out again but then the bird flew away, with a crack of the branches and a rush of the leaves on next door's tree. Too late. He'd never know what it was now. Mirrie would have known.

But Mirrie's head was buried in her computer. It had been ever since lockdown. He couldn't believe a person had that much work to do. She surely didn't work that hard when she'd been going to the office, not from what she talked about when she got home, on the relatively rare occasions they were together. Sundays mostly. She never mentioned her work. All she did talk about was the colour of the suit Sam had been wearing that day, and whether or not Molly from accounts was having an affair with Sandra from HR. How she managed now, working from home, with nothing to gossip about, was a puzzle.

He knew he irritated her, being around all the time. It was not his fault. He was assistant manager of a night club in Shoreditch. Sounded glamorous, but it wasn't. It was a mix of security officer, health and safety and crowd control. But it was a job, and now he was furloughed, on 80% of his pay, with nothing to do all day. And no way of knowing once the furlough ended whether or not he'd still have a job at the end of it. He tried not to think about it, what was the point?

So there was the business of filling the day. Keith did not find this as much of a problem as he expected. He had no compunction to learn a new trade, or language, or hobby, let alone to leap out of bed first thing and do press-ups. He was an ambition-free person who was perfectly content to lounge around doing not very much. It would have been more fun if Mirrie had done some of the lounging with him. He'd half hoped all this time together at home meant time together, but Mirrie obviously didn't see things that way. There was always Netflix however. Time passed reasonably enough.

So was she coming or wasn't she? Did she not hear him? She must have heard him – all the doors were open. Was she deliberately ignoring him? Were those numbers and facts and figures so absorbing she didn't want to be disturbed? Or was she Trying To Make a Point? Yes, that was probably it. But what exactly was the Point she was trying to make?

It was beyond him.

He decided to go for a walk. A very long walk.

~

'Mirrie, come and look at this!'

Miranda hesitated. She was in the middle of a particularly complicated set of data-crunching, moving items from column to column, from spreadsheet to spreadsheet. It was taking her longer than usual because, typically, her mind kept wandering and she kept having to go back over stuff.

'What is it?' she yelled back.

'This!' said Keith.

This. Oh well. She got heavily to her feet – whatever it was it had better be good – and joined her husband in the garden. It was a tiny garden, barely big enough to hold anything exciting.

'What is it?' she asked.

He was gazing upwards, his hand shading his eyes against the sun, pointing at next door's tree.

'There,' he said.

'Where?'

'There, just above the . . . there, in the branches.'

'What exactly am I looking at?'

'Can't you see it? The green thing?'

At which point, with a whoosh and a great shaking of the branches of next door's tree a huge, brightly-coloured bird emerged and flew off.

'That?' said Miranda, in disbelief.

'Yes, that.'

'It was a parakeet. A bloody parakeet. Have you never seen a parakeet before?'

Keith shook his head. He looked quite bewildered, and yet excited too, like a small child.

'Oh, Keith.'

'What?'

'They're everywhere.'

'Are they?'

'They're a scourge.'

'They're never!'

'Absolutely. They bully the smaller birds, they force their way onto the bird feeders, steal all the best spots for their nests!'

'Do they?' He looked distinctly crestfallen.

'Is that what you called me out to see?'

He nodded.

'Is that what you interrupted my work for?'

He nodded again, and formed his mouth into what looked for all the world like a pout.

'Oh, Keith.' She held out her arms and, like a small boy, he allowed himself to be enveloped in them.

Now and then

They were the best years in living memory.

It was the time of the pill but before HIV Aids. We had the Beach Boys and Crosby Stills and Nash but no Young, and every Simon and Garfunkel song was written especially for us. We sauntered around without a bra yet still expected the guys to open doors for us. Best of all we had endless sunshine in this adopted country of ours, beneath which we would spread our skimpily-clad, eager and unprotected bodies for hours on end on any one of an endless number of beaches; and when it got truly unbearable we'd plunge our sizzling selves into the surf and allow it to toss us about like flotsam before slamming us down onto the rock-hard sand; this in the days before we learned respect for the ocean we never understood.

At weekends when the beaches got too crowded we crammed into our cars and drove a couple of hours – in any direction so long as it was north or south and hugged the coast – till we found a beach we could have to ourselves, where we'd strip off and skinny-dip till the cows came home and the stars came out.

In the evenings there was rum and coke, or brandy and ginger ale, and a rotgut wine that came in a box. We rolled illegal but largely innocuous substances in cigarette papers and drifted off to la-la land; and on flush days when we felt we could afford it we'd eat out Italian or Greek or Lebanese. Somewhere in the midst of it all we reluctantly held down jobs of one sort or another, usually temporary, badly paid but happily commitment free.

We were aware that somewhere to the west of us lay a vast and empty continent of desert, scrub and interminable boringness. And on occasion we'd venture forth to stop off at one of the one-horse towns we found so terribly amusing and laugh at the yokels who glowered at us over their beers. We heard stories of locals who'd never travelled further than twenty miles from their home town and had barely heard of the nation's cities, let alone the great Abroad, and we took it in turns – the yokels and us – to see who could scoff longest and loudest at the worlds we knew nothing about.

It wasn't all fun and laughter, of course, but it was difficult to be sad for too long amid the effortless beauty of a country where winding roads took us high above the clifftops overlooking the wild ocean, and where the water of the harbour peeked unexpectedly between the edges of the city buildings. There was water everywhere you looked – the harbour for boating and swimming (and sharks) and the ocean for sailing and surfing (and sharks). It was a country to be young in, a country to be a bum in, and we fulfilled both of these to the manner born.

And then, two weeks before I was due to leave Jamie appeared.

We'd been to a show he was in and a bunch of us came back to my place afterwards, and one by one they peeled off until it was just him and me. And if I hadn't drunk half a box of the rotgut I probably would have panicked at being alone in the room in the middle of the night with the 1970s version of Brad Pitt: local star, golden blonde hair, big smile, amused eyes, I knew him from his television shows – everyone did – but I would never have guessed in a million years we would end up right here, just the two of us.

We talked through the night. He was the first actor I'd ever met who didn't talk endlessly about himself. Actually come to think of it he did talk about himself, but it was an unusually interesting self, a farming self. At the age of 21 he'd just bought an orchard that he ran as a business with a friend. He described in great detail how they grew the apples and nurtured them and then harvested them. Of how they set off into the bush with tractor and chainsaw and came back with rafters and beams for the kitchen they were building, working together in silence because they knew one another so well they could anticipate each other's every move without a word spoken. To a townie like me it was romantic beyond belief and for the first time in all those years in my adopted country I understood the proper definition of 'mateship'.

I told him I never went to bed with a man the first time I'd met him but he didn't seem to hear me. So the rest of that night was the first of many, but not many enough. We tore the clothes off one another's smooth-skinned, taut bodies and made love quickly and urgently and rather earnestly. There wasn't a lot of foreplay – there wasn't any foreplay – and there was none of the gentle manipulation of secret spots that we had yet to learn about.

Oh heady days! But I'd packed my bags all ready to leave and I was waiting for him to say, 'Don't go' or even 'I wish you weren't going', but he didn't. And knowing how I was in those days I would probably have gone anyway no matter what he said, because I was an independent woman who did not allow men to dictate the course of her life. Not then anyway.

~

Years passed, as years do. I kept in touch and from time to time he responded. We wrote long and passionate letters to one another saying how we longed to see each other again. He told me how on rainy days he and his friend would sit inside and make toy trucks out of oregano that smelled wondrous when freshly cut, and racing cars from red cedar that smelt like curry. Then on a whim he sold the orchard and bought a farm and became a proper farmer. We met up again when we were visiting one another's countries and between times I yearned and pined and wrote sonnets comparing him (favourably) with Greek gods. In time we married – other people – and had children. I continued to think about him now and again. Many years later our marriages began to falter and then to disintegrate altogether. And so I went back to his country to be with him again.

No, that was not the reason. I was writing a book about his country, about the history of his country, and it was the research that took me back there. The sun still shone and the water of the harbour still sparkled in between the buildings, though not so much now those buildings were larger and closer together. The beaches were more crowded and less easy to get to and park at, but by then the idea of lying on the sand all day was not so appealing. There was food now from every country in the world – Thailand, Malaysia, Vietnam, Korea – and the wine came in proper bottles with screw-tops and actually tasted respectable.

The magnificent coastline was still there but this time my work took me inland, to the endless scrub and the beleaguered one-horse towns we used to laugh at, where the heart of the country lay. It was here that I discovered dark stories of the country's colonial past, of the ravage of the countryside and of its original inhabitants by usurping westerners, how it became known as the lucky country where the whole world wanted to move to. But the whole world was no longer welcome and illegal visitors were incarcerated sometimes for years on offshore islands. The people who not that long ago had been paid to go there were closing the doors behind them.

All this I hadn't known in the old days. Or perhaps I just wasn't interested. It didn't seem relevant, or necessary.

~

It was infatuation, I did know that. After all I hardly knew Jamie and in my deepest sensible heart I suspected we would not have lasted the course, it was just that the course had been interrupted before we had a chance to find out. I'd been seduced and infatuated by him as I'd been by his country. But I was older and wiser now, wasn't I?

He hadn't aged that well. He'd lost a good deal of his hair and he'd grown a bit of a belly. I often pondered if I met him at this age if I'd have still found him attractive. I discovered other things about him too – he had a ruthless streak, and he was secretive. He had given up acting but he was a farmer still, and a businessman. He drank too much and he was bad at communicating.

His body wasn't taut any more and his skin was no longer smooth. But then mine was no great shakes either, dotted with cellulite, and moles, yet it seemed not to matter. I somehow didn't mind him seeing my naked body and he didn't seem to mind it either. Love-making was shall we say relaxed, yet still passionate. We touched each other in places we knew we really liked, in the secret spots we didn't know about way back when. On occasion a touch of cramp or a recalcitrant limb had us collapsing into helpless laughter, and I was reminded of my mother's description of my father playing tennis in his latter years: making up for his lack of athleticism with technique and cunning.

By now Jamie had firmly descended from the pedestal I'd placed him on. He'd lost his Greek god status and had come to join the rest of us ordinary mortals. Like his country he had exposed his flaws – or more to the point, I had opened my eyes to them. His country may have had a doubtful background but no more so than anywhere else, just more recently and better chronicled. It was still the most beautiful place on earth.

And so for some reason which will remain unfathomable, in my so-called maturity I loved them both as deeply and passionately – more, because through their flaws they were humanised – as I ever did.

Two halves, one whole

1

If Ellie had lived any closer to Aunt Vee things might have turned out very differently. As it was the length of time it took her to get from one place to the other was exactly the time it took for her idea to germinate and still seem like a good idea – no, an excellent idea, so much so she wondered why she hadn't thought of it before – but not yet time enough for her to give it proper consideration and therefore to realise, like so many ideas that seem so promising in their infancy, that it was no such thing.

Possibly a bit of her was aware of this as she rang the doorbell because she found herself speaking even before she'd properly stepped over the threshold.

'I've had an idea, Vee. While I'm away. I'm going to ask Jason to come and look after you.'

'*Jason?* He can't even look after himself.' With which Aunt Vee turned her back on her niece and limped in her lopsided fashion down the hallway.

'That's my point,' Ellie called after her. 'It would do him good and you too.'

'You think so.' Aunt Vee was in the kitchen now, boiling the kettle. She was still quietly fuming over the fact that her niece was going away in the first place – not because she didn't deserve it, because she did, and some, or because she, Vee, would be without a carer for a month – but because it irked her that it mattered.

Ellie was not going to be deflected. Now the idea was out it was going to be made to work.

'If you think about it it makes total sense. Two people who need looking after and I'm not going to be there to look after either of them and therefore: ergo, it makes sense that you look after one another'.

There was a dense silence as Aunt Vee filled the coffee pot, fetched the mugs, placed them on the kitchen table, filled the milk jug. She walked with a list now, favouring the good hip over the dodgy one, which she hated as it made her look like a clown and small children laughed at her in the street and called her a hobbit.

They sat at the kitchen table and drank their coffee, still in silence.

It was years since Ellie had had a proper break and it was only by dint of some forceful persuasion on the part of her brother, who lived with his family in San Francisco, that she was daring to take one now. Her brother, being a man, had little idea what it meant to just take off when there were people who were dependent on you, one of them your mentally ill son and the other your increasingly disabled elderly aunt. Although as her brother had pointed out this 'apparent' (his word) dependency pretty well meant Ellie was doomed to spend the rest of her life going nowhere.

It had occurred to Ellie that between the two halves of them – the son with the active body but dysfunctioning mind and the elderly relative with the quicksilver mind but faltering body – there was every reason why the one should not complement the other to form one complete whole. That was the logical conclusion if not the practical one.

'I thought you said Jason had agoraphobia,' said Vee

sullenly, after a long while.

'I think that's probably in his head. If he . . .'

'Ha!' said Vee. It was not meant unkindly, though it sounded like it, and it was marginally less aggressive than the thought, unspoken, *'I told you as much'*.

'If he had a reason,' Ellie persisted. 'The reason he doesn't leave home is because he thinks there's no need. And the longer he doesn't leave home the harder it gets. That's what I mean by it being good for him.'

'Hmm.' Vee drank her coffee and placed her mug down on the table and clasped her gnarled hands together. 'I don't want to spoil your chance of a break, certainly not on my account. I will be perfectly all right on my own – how long will you be gone for?'

'A month.'

'That's nothing. I will be perfectly all right. There is no need to bother Jason.'

'Of course there is. What about your shopping?'

'I'll stock up.'

'It's far too long for you to survive without shopping. Vee I mean this, Jason is perfectly capable of at least being on hand to do whatever's required. It will do him a certain amount of good to think of someone else for a change.'

You can say that again, thought the old woman.

2

Aunt Vee, real name Veronica Simpkins, one of three sisters, had spent her working life as a civil servant, mostly at the Foreign Office, in one of those low-key yet essential jobs without which no office can function, and which she performed in such a low-key manner that few people were aware she was doing it in the first place. She pretended this did not bother her and since she had been brought up never to draw attention to herself she continued with her tasks quietly and without complaint, excusing her cowardice – for she was more than once overlooked for promotion – by managing to convince herself she held the rational (and stoical) high ground.

She was a bright girl, and not unattractive, if a bit standoffish, and while marriage and motherhood had never been part of her life plan – insofar as she had one – when she reached the age of forty and neither of them was showing the slightest sign of taking place, she felt a moment of despondency. But then her rational self reminded her that since she did not actually like children – they were messy, unpredictable and got in the way – it was probably all to the good.

She was retired at sixty, which was now twenty-five years ago and far too young for a woman of her intellect and ability. She'd spent the years since then living off her modest but adequate pension (she had been brought up to be frugal) and keeping her mind alert through classes in medieval history and Renaissance art, going on organised trips to places like Florence with like-minded people – or what she hoped would be like-minded people but who turned out actually to be interested far more in Italian food and gossip than Titian and Michelangelo – and one way or another she had filled in the time quite satisfactorily, if not exactly joyously.

Ellie, the daughter of her elder and now late sister, was her nearest relative, and insofar as Vee was capable of loving anyone she sort of loved Ellie, who was a kind soul, far too kind in fact, who indulged – in Vee's opinion – her wastrel son beyond imagining and always had done. And now, since she'd got it into her head that he was clinically and mentally ill it seemed to Vee that Ellie was allowing him to get away with absolutely everything; when the truth as she saw it was that Jason had since a very early age, certainly ever since his father walked out on them all those years ago, managed to twist his mother around his little finger to a degree that made Vee's blood boil.

So there was a good deal of unspoken angst in the relationship between Ellie and her aunt, of which both were aware. Thus it was that in a moment of clarity, having committed herself to her month away, Ellie had blithely and perhaps over-enthusiastically decided that this arrangement, this putting together of two broken halves to create a complete whole, was not only a useful one practically but might go some way to mending the breach between the two most important people in her life.

3

Jason had always been a troubled boy. His teacher had called him 'the least motivated child it has ever been my doubtful pleasure to have taught'. Quite early on he was diagnosed with ADHD, or perhaps that should be ADD, since hyperactivity had never been Jason's problem. He was given medication that didn't really work, and so he drifted through school and emerged at the age of sixteen with no qualifications, no direction and no ambition. He held down a few jobs stacking shelves and even at one point working in a bar before being sacked, usually for being late or 'slow'. Well-meaning friends tried from time to time to help out with casual jobs – clearing their gardens or their lofts – but as often as not he didn't turn up, and when he did, he tended to disappear before completing the job.

And now recently he had taken to his room and at the age of twenty he'd been diagnosed with some mental disorder which did not seem to have a specific name but involved paranoia, agoraphobia and various other socio-phobic ailments. He was prescribed medication which Ellie claimed made a difference but which he, Jason, asserted did not, which is why he often refused to take it.

For Ellie it was unimaginably lonely. She had always

believed in unconditional love and something deep-rooted inside her told her that was all that was needed to bring Jason round. Friends implied she was soft on him and hard on herself. Others, usually behind her back, claimed she was terrified of the prospect of living without him and that his 'problems' had been, if not invented, then exaggerated by his mother in order to keep him with her. Whether there was any truth in any of there was absolutely no way anyone could persuade Ellie to change course now. Consistency, she insisted, was crucial.

The day before Ellie flew to San Francisco she did a mammoth shop for Vee and watched while Jason, not without complaint, changed his bedding and washed both it and his clothes. She made both of her charges promise to call each other at least once every other day. They in turn insisted they would do this and that she was not to give them a thought, they would be absolutely fine without her. She should forget all about them for a month and have a jolly good time with her brother and his family.

4

Jason's world was his bedroom. The walls and the ceiling were his sky, the floor his oceans and continents, his battlefields and warzones, the bed his retreat. The battlefields were strewn quite naturally with the detritus of combat: discarded clothes, empty soft drink cans, old magazines and other things you wouldn't want to look too closely at.

Wars had been fought and won in this room, regimes toppled, insurgents sent packing and terrorists terrorised single-handedly. This was a secure world, the world of fighters and heroes, safer and infinitely less frightening than the actual world beyond the door. The conduit to it, the phone, rang from time to and time and was ignored while more important matters were attended to. Likewise the doorbell, that on this particular morning buzzed and buzzed and buzzed, so interfering with Jason's virtual existence that in the end it too had to be attended to.

There, on the doorstep, leaning on a stick and breathing heavily, stood an elderly woman with a familiar face.

'Can I help you?' he said.

'You do know who I am?' said the old woman, rather crossly.

'Auntie Vee!'

'Where have you been?' She was panting a bit. 'I've been trying to contact you for a week. You were supposed to keep in touch.'

Jason said nothing.

'Well?' She paused momentarily for breath and continued to glare at him. 'Are you going to let me in?'

'Of course.' And he stepped aside in the doorway politely, like a butler.

'So, what have you been up to? Other than not answering your telephone?'

Without waiting for the answer – a habit of Auntie Vee's – the elderly woman hobbled down the hallway to the living room, reminding Jason for a chronic moment of a hobbit.

She pushed open a door and stifled a shriek. 'And what do you call this?'

'The living room.'

She turned to look at him sharply and he gazed back at her wide-eyed beneath his mop of uncut, unruly and obviously unwashed hair.

'We had an arrangement I believe.' She waited for a response. 'But you failed to keep your side of it.'

'Did I? Sorry Auntie Vee.'

'Yes, well. So what have you been up to?' she repeated, as she pushed open the door to his bedroom. 'Good God! Is this how you normally live?'

He frowned. He couldn't immediately see why his bedroom or the way he lived his life in it could be anyone else's business, least of all his aunt's.

'Phoo!' She waved her hand in front of her face. 'Do you ever open a window?'

Why would he want to open a window? What did windows or what lay beyond them have to do with anything? But the hobbit was picking her way through the warzone, reaching out and struggling to open the window that had not been opened since the Wayzak rebel army defeated the state troops in the battle of Zanzikan.

She gave up and all but lost her balance. He reached out to steady her and she shrugged him off.

'And your socks need darning.'

'What's darning?'

'Oh for goodness' sake!'

The rebels were coming up on the right flank, in her blind spot. Kazow! Another regime falls.

'May I please sit down?' she panted.

'Of course.' There was a pause, as he stood there vacantly. 'Be my guest.'

The old woman gazed pointedly around the room.

He shoved aside some of the debris on his bed, his country. And she sat, gingerly.

'So Jason, what are we going to do?' She sighed.

The enemy wants to negotiate. Tread carefully.

'Do?'

'We are supposed to be looking after one another. I think you should come and stay with me.'

Non-negotiable.

'Pack up some things. You can come back later and clear up.'

Enemy's terms chronically unacceptable.

'Did you hear me?'

She was getting flustered now. Flustered and cross.

'Oh for goodness' sake. Get some things together, you're coming with me.'

'I'm what?'

It wasn't, as it happens, what Aunt Vee had intended to say. She had called on Jason not because she particularly wanted to see him, far from it, but because she was so utterly furious that the lad had not made the *slightest* effort to keep the promise he had so solemnly made to his mother a week ago. Not only was he not answering his own telephone he was making no attempt to return his aunt's calls; which was, in her book, the ultimate in bad manners and something with which no one, young or old, should be allowed to get away, no matter how apparently mentally ill they purported to be.

'Come on, I have a taxi waiting outside.'

'Why do you want me to go with you?' Said politely, to humour the enemy.

'Because you cannot be trusted, and because you have broken your promise to your mother. And because I cannot be expected to keep making the journey here in order to see whether or not you are alive.' With which, as was her wont, Aunt Vee heaved herself to her feet, exited the room and was through the front door to the waiting taxi before Jason had time to articulate his side of the deal.

Ten minutes later she was still waiting. The front door stood open and behind it, out of her sight, on the floor, sat Jason, rocking back and forth.

A man appeared in the doorway, a stranger.

'Come on son,' said the cab driver. 'The old lady's getting cold. And a bit, you know.' He leant down to help Jason to his feet and the lad recoiled.

'Look,' the driver was getting impatient now. 'I haven't got all day and nor has the old lady, even if you have.'

With which the burly stranger grabbed the young man under the armpit and hauled him to his feet. 'Got your things?' he asked.

The lad started to keen. It was an unearthly sound, like a wild animal in distress, and now it was the driver who recoiled.

'I'll get them.'

The kid strode to his room and collected up his life support system: his war machines, his sound machines, one pair of trousers and one of socks, and before he had a moment to realise what he was doing he had turned his back on his virtual world and plunged himself headlong into the great wild unknown.

'Front door!' called his nemesis, from the back of the cab. 'And don't forget the keys!'

Keys were found, front door slammed shut. The enemy, for the moment, was in command. For the moment.

5

A day later Ellie received an email from her aunt with the news that Jason was now staying with her until his mother's return, to which she reacted with a mixture of horror and disbelief, and only by the skin of her teeth did she stop herself from replying, 'Please don't bully him'.

6

If he tidied himself up a bit he was not a bad-looking boy, thought Aunt Vee, even if he was a half-and-half. He had a useless father who pushed off when Jason was – she forgot exactly how old – young enough to miss his dad, who since the separation had chosen to take not the slightest interest in his son.

The extraordinary thing about modern parents, mused the mother of none, was how they allowed their children to dictate to them. To 85-year-old Aunt Vee this was a total reversal of the natural order of things and went some way to explaining What was Wrong with Modern Youth Today. Her own parents had been of the old order who lay down strict rules which, even though she might not always have agreed with them, or even complied with them, meant above all the young Vee always knew what was what.

Vee had risen at 7.30am every day of her working life, and since her retirement she had allowed herself a half hour sleep-in, which didn't make a lot of sense since she was invariably awake anyway at 7am but it made her feel just slightly indulgent. In years past she'd got up to make herself a cup of tea and taken it back to bed to drink it; but now that the effort of actually getting up was so taxing she'd foregone that little treat. With Jason in the house however there was the possibility of reinstating it.

When Jason did not emerge from his room on the first day of his stay Aunt Vee went from annoyance to rage to concern and back to annoyance, all in the space of one morning. She tapped and then hammered on his door and when she eventually managed to shove it open (he hadn't deliberately barricaded himself in, it was just where his clothes had fallen the night before) she couldn't get any response out of him at all. So he stayed put in his bedroom and did not emerge once, even – to Vee's consternation – to go to the bathroom.

7

Jason first became aware of his halitosis after a passing remark of his mother's following a particularly heavy night out with his friends. He was 16 years old. To be precise he was not so much with friends as tagging along and doing everything they did, in excess, in an attempt – unsuccessfully – to ingratiate himself. 'Good God you smell like a sack of rotting potatoes!' she'd told him, flapping her hands up and down to emphasise the point. It

72

was her way of encouraging him to clean his teeth and to wash occasionally rather than rely on pharmaceutical products to mask the bodily odours. It was then that he realised why it was people kept their distance in crowded places and avoided sitting next to him on the underground.

The doctor told him there was nothing wrong, he put his nose right up to Jason's mouth and told him to breathe out and didn't even flinch when he did, but Jason knew he was lying. He told Jason bad breath was often due to a form of gum disease, so Jason asked if there was an operation to cure it and the doctor just laughed. He got the same response from the dentist. 'Your breath smells? You should see some of the mouths I have to put up with!' But Jason still wasn't convinced. If it wasn't bad breath that kept people away then it would have to be something worse. So he took to gum and mints and mouthwash, he even took to drinking the mouthwash neat, which once you got used to it was quite tasty actually. But still people avoided him and even on occasion gave him disgusted looks.

8

She found him first thing the following morning. He was standing in the middle of her sitting room attired in a tatty tee shirt and grubby boxer shorts, gazing around as if he hadn't the faintest idea where he was.

'So you've joined the living at last.'

'What am I doing here?' he asked.

'You're staying with me, don't you remember? Good gracious. And where were you all yesterday, you didn't come out of your room once.'

'I want to go home,' said the boy, and he started to tremble.

'Well you can't.' Clever lad, he could look vulnerable

and terrified all at once without the least effort. 'We have a pact. And now you can make yourself breakfast. You can do such a thing, can you not?'

'Uhhhh.' It was an odd sound, belonging more to a kid half his age.

'In there.' She was not going to be deflected. 'Kettle. Coffee. Tea. Mugs. Cornflakes.' She gestured toward the kitchen. 'But first,' she went on, 'a bath. Or a shower. Whichever you prefer. You know where the bathroom is? You'll find a towel in the cupboard.'

And she turned and went.

It was a strategy she'd adopted without any particular forethought but she instinctively knew the moment she began to humour him, to stop and ask him not to make that dreadful noise or, God forbid, to ask him what was the matter, all would be lost.

And her strategy worked. When she knew he didn't think she was watching him she saw him entering the bathroom and emerging soon after looking damp (promising); after which he got dressed (in the same clothes he'd arrived in) and went into the kitchen, from where she heard faint banging noises and where, a short while later, she found him sitting with a mug of something hot on the table in front of him, gazing into space.

All of which went to prove, in Aunt Vee's mind, that there was nothing really wrong with the young man at all.

'I have made out a shopping list,' she said as she presented him with scrap of A4 paper neatly torn into four. 'There's a Sainsbury's five minutes down the road on the right hand side. I hope you can read my writing. My eyesight is not what it was.'

He looked blankly first at her and then at her list. He shoved his hands between his knees and scrutinised the piece of paper for a very long time before looking up at her.

'What do you want me to do?'

'I want you . . .' she stopped, settled, and tried to shut out the annoyance. 'I would like you to do my shopping for me. Please. There's a supermarket down the road, on the right hand side, you can't miss it.'

'How big is it?' he asked.

'How big is what?'

'The supermarket.'

'I . . . it's medium-sized I suppose. What do you mean?'

'Square metreage, exactly. I'm not allowed anywhere that's more than 100 square metres.'

'Not allowed? What are you talking about?'

'Agoraphobia. Only small supermarkets, corner shops, that sort of thing.'

'Oh good God!'

'You'll have corner shops. They'll have all this.'

'I don't want corner shops! I want fresh produce. Fresh and cheap and, well, Sainsbury's.'

'Support your local shops.'

'What is this, a political statement?'

'Mr Khan and his family. They know me. They've run the corner shop since I was a kid.'

'You can't go there, it's miles away!'

'I'll find it.'

And he was out of the house before she could stop him.

9

The following day Jason offered to cook his aunt a cake. It was something he was seriously good at, he told her, everyone said so. He was better at making cakes than his mother, better than anyone she knew even, she had told him as much many times. And while Aunt Vee was not fond of cakes, except perhaps for a very innocuous Victoria sponge, she didn't want to dampen his enthusiasm so she nodded and said, 'It's all yours', pointing at the kitchen, and heaving a small sigh as she started to negotiate the staircase.

'You should have your bed brought down here,' he called up at her when she was halfway up.

'I beg your pardon?'

'Bring your bed down here. Then you wouldn't have to worry about the stairs.'

'What are you talking about?'

'You're an old woman, old women can't climb stairs, everyone knows that.'

'If I want . . .' Aunt Vee clutched onto the banisters to balance herself. 'If I want to bring my bed down to the ground floor I will do it. And I may be old, and decrepit, but I can still manage a flight of stairs, thank you.'

'Just a thought.'

Oh God, thought Aunt Vee. What a ridiculous way to behave.

The cake was not a success. It came out soft and mushy, so he put it back in the oven for another fifteen minutes, and then another ten, making a total of sixty minutes altogether, and the end result was as dry and tasteless as cotton wool. And Jason began to cry.

'It's only a cake,' said his aunt, but quite gently. He had tried, and been so proud.

'I'm the best cake-maker. I can make cakes, ma says I could sell them if I wanted to.'

'Cakes are strange things. Sometimes they work and sometimes they just don't.'

'What would you know?'

'I . . . Well.'

And that was the end of that conversation.

10

She asked him one day why he ate with a hand in front of

his mouth. She had assumed it was a form of politeness, or maybe that he was embarrassed to eat in front of other people. But his response was totally unexpected.

'My breath smells.'

'Nonsense,' she said.

'They all say that!'

'Keep your voice down Jason.'

'Nobody believes me. They pretend to but they don't. You don't know what it's like! You don't know what it's like when people avoid you, all the time.'

'Because you have bad breath?'

'You ever tried to kiss a girl with bad breath? No?'

Vee couldn't help herself.

'Laugh, yes, go on! Laugh away! Very funny!'

'I hadn't noticed, I promise you. You do not have bad breath.'

'You too!' At which Jason slammed down his knife and fork and exited the room.

11

He missed his bedroom at home. It was where his world was and his new place wasn't the same, no matter how hard he tried. For a start Aunt Vee insisted he clear his stuff up every day, which wasn't how his world worked. His world did not begin afresh each new day and wind itself up neatly at the end of it. Conflicts were not like that. You try telling a bunch of stroppy insurgents, 'Time to clear up now'.

You were meant to live in the world with other people, to communicate with them, to share things, talk about things, on some kind of mutual level. He would never try to engage his aunt in conversation about Matrix IV or the advantages of the X-Box over the PS4. So why she should rabbit on about Churchill and the War and expect him to pay attention made no sense, she was not keeping her side of the bargain, and to simply say 'you should take an interest' was chronically meaningless. As for the 'ignorance of modern youth', which was a favourite phrase of hers and which she could bang on about for twenty minutes, it was all he could do not to commit physical violence. And how she could go on and on and on about the 'vacuousness' – another favourite word – of modern times and then have the nerve to tell him off whenever he said 'give us a break', which he said quite often, admittedly, was just chronically unfair. And just because Jason lacked the words or the self-control to articulate his side of things as well as he might have done meant she won every argument hands down, or thought she did. And this really really riled.

12

There was one time when Jason did come near to actual physical violence.

It wasn't until the third week that the April weather turned mild enough for Vee to suggest an excursion to the local park. It was the thing she missed more than anything now she felt so unsteady on her feet, and the macular degeneration that meant she could only really see anything if she looked at it sideways added to her feelings of insecurity. Within her own house it was different, memory did much of the seeing for her, but outside was different.

The five minute journey, with Jason bumbling along beside her, head down, eyes fixed on the pavement, took nearly half an hour; partly because she had asked him, please, for her safety's sake, not to plug himself into whatever it was he habitually plugged himself into on this occasion because she needed him to be her eyes and ears as well as her prop, to which he had shrugged and agreed with extremely bad grace and made a point of dragging his feet to press the point.

But here they were at last, safely in the café, albeit coffee- and tea-less because Jason had refused, on some pretext to do with being unable to talk to strangers, to venture to the counter to buy any. But the day was mild and still and there was the scent of blossom in the air.

'The magnolia must be out round about now,' said Vee. It was meant to be a question, but when Jason did not respond. 'Well? You are my eyes, Jason.'

He shrugged.

'Please tell me. Tell me what you see.'

Jason looked around vaguely.

'Trees,' he said.

'Yes?'

'Grass. Kids.'

'Is the magnolia in blossom? It's across the lawn there, opposite the shed.'

Jason looked and shrugged. He was still in a sulk. The interior world that he plugged himself into was more than a distraction from the outside world, it *was* his world.

'Oh good heavens, you haven't got the courtesy to answer a simple question. I blame your father.'

The statement, coming out of the blue as it did, hung in the air for some time. The more Jason did not respond the angrier Aunt Vee became.

'He was a ship that passed in the night, you do know that.'

Jason mumbled something inaudible.

'She should have had an abortion.'

She could sense him stiffening and added hastily (even she knew that was going too far), 'That's not to say you were not wanted. You were. But it wasn't fair on you, or on Ellie. Every boy needs a father. Someone to look up to. Someone to steer them on the right path. Not that the path your father chose was something you would want to emulate.'

'My dad's okay,' said Jason, though to tell the truth he knew remarkably little about him. He had a vague recollection of a tall, big man with very white teeth, and he'd seen photos, once.

'Oh? When did you last see him?'

Jason did not reply.

'These people,' she began. 'They have no idea. Why your mother should get caught up with such . . .'

'What do you mean, these people?'

'You know what I mean.'

'Say it then.' Jason's knee was jerking so violently the table between them was shaking.

'These people. Black people. You know perfectly well what I mean.'

'That's racist.'

'Well you explain it then. You tell me what's going on in these African countries where the people are starving to death. They haven't the faintest idea.'

'What's that got to do with my father?'

'I'm not talking about your father, he was from Jamaica. But they're all the same.'

Jason stood up so suddenly he knocked his chair over.

'You bitch!' He was shouting. 'You bastard! Bitch! You . . .!'

'Jason for goodness' sake . . .'

'You take that back!'

'Look, I didn't mean . . .' She looked over his shoulder and through the blur she could see people were turning to stare.

'He never did me any harm! Not at all! You don't know! You don't fucking . . .'

'Hey, what's going on?'

It was the guy from the café, with apron and pony tail.

'What are you saying?' He went to stand rather too

close to Jason and eyeballed him.

'It's all right.' Aunt Vee reached out a placatory hand. 'Look, it was my fault, I shouldn't have . . . It was my fault. It's perfectly all right.'

To her astonishment what Aunt Vee wanted to do more than anything was take the trembling body of her great-nephew into her arms and give him a very big hug. But Jason had gone somewhere unreachable. As the café manager retreated, with a backward glance, the boy continued to stand there, still shaking, fists and teeth clenched, eyes fixed on something down and to the side of him that was probably not there. She reached out to touch his arm and he flinched.

She was afraid he might just walk off and leave her. Her dependence and utter powerlessness terrified her, but what frightened her most was her impending loss of identity: a realisation that at her time of life, with all her knowledge, experience and wisdom, she was being forced into a position where she had to curb her tongue.

Jason did not walk off and leave her because whether or not he was aware of it he was as dependent on Aunt Vee to get him home as she was on him.

13

The experience unnerved Vee so much that she spent her afternoon nap time lying on her bed staring wide-eyed at the ceiling and thinking.

Her father had always defined violence as the last resort of the barbarian. He believed passionately in the power of the spoken word and its ability to solve pretty well any problem known to mankind; that it was only the inability of the world's leaders to argue their case over the negotiating table that led to wars and conflict. This conviction extended to the home, which is why on occasion when Vee, as a schoolgirl, came home from school in a sulk he would take her firmly by the arm, sit her down and say, 'Tell me the problem.'

What may or may not have worked for world leaders was in the case of a stroppy fourteen-year-old – who even if she did know the cause of this particular sulk was unable to articulate it – inevitably pretty much a failure. But her father was persistent: there was no letting go until she at least made an attempt to analyse herself. 'Everything has a cause,' he said. 'And every problem a solution. Let us talk it through.'

To say that Jason was inarticulate was so much of an understatement it was barely worth mentioning.

When she tried to recall exactly what he had said at the moment of confrontation that morning all that came to mind were insults and meaningless phrases such as 'You take that back!'. Not once did Jason offer any concrete reason why he should defend the father who had walked out on him.

It made no sense at all to Vee that a boy like Jason should feel so strongly about an absent and negligent father while taking the mother who'd devoted her life to him so totally for granted. Not being a parent she was not to know this was a not uncommon scenario within families, as in life generally: the love you want is the love you can't have. What it did confirm in Vee's already mostly made-up mind was the danger of unconditional love. If you know your mother, or your father, will love you no matter what you do and forgive you for everything, where is the incentive in trying to better yourself?

14

'What the fuck?'

'I won't have that language in this house.'

'Okay, then I'll leave.'

'You will not.'

'As soon as you give me back my stuff.'

Aunt Vee gave Jason her most withering look. 'I have no intention . . .'

'What fucking right? Eh? It's my private property!'

He was standing in the doorway of his temporary bedroom, hands on hips, breathing rather heavily. Vee was not intimidated.

'Confiscated, perhaps. I have every right.'

'Why? Fuck why?'

She flinched every time he said the word. 'I am trying to prove a . . .'

'What?'

'If you will let me speak.'

'I don't care why. Give the fucking stuff back.'

'You just asked . . . '

'Give – the – fucking – stuff – back. Are you deaf?'

'I will not . . .' Vee swallowed hard and looked him straight in the eye. 'I took them for a reason, if you want to know. Which you say you don't.'

She waited.

'It is my opinion that those – toys – are partly the cause of your problem,' she said.

'What fucking problem?'

'You have just articulated it. To begin with the fact that you seem unable to form a sentence that does not contain a four-letter expletive.'

'What the fuck's that got to do with anything?'

'Come and sit down, Jason.'

'I don't want to sit down.'

'I took them because I want you to communicate.' She was speaking loudly now. 'To communicate with me, in the real world, rather than in . . .' She waved her hands in the direction of the bedroom in which, until an hour before, the recently-removed articles had been sheltering.

'Whatever it is you call it. Your virtual world. Where nothing is real. It's not healthy, and it's not sociable, or friendly. And it does you no good.'

'Says?'

'In my opinion.'

'Well that's your . . . it's fucking chronic.'

'And that's another thing. What precisely do you mean by the word "chronic"?'

'Chronic. You know.'

'The word "chronic", according to the dictionary, means persistent. As in a persistent headache, one that persists, as opposed to acute, which is . . .'

But he'd turned back into his room and slammed the door.

15

One of the rules Vee had laid down was that they eat one meal a day together, at the table, during which they would hold a conversation.

Conversation, to Jason – had he been asked, which he hadn't – was pointless unless people had something to say, something that was interesting, which most of the time it wasn't. It had driven him mad the way his mum pretended to be interested in people she hardly knew, like 'How's the family?' to the Polish guy at the newsagents who she didn't even like, she told him as much. 'It's the oil that keeps the world turning,' she used to say, which didn't make sense either.

None of Vee's good conversational intentions had led to anything much until tonight. Mostly it was chatter – what kind of TV programmes did he like, and what exactly was The Voice? And did he ever read a book? And even Jason knew she didn't give a toss whether he read a book or not, what she was really saying is 'Why don't you read a book?'

This occasion was different however. Now there was something he really wanted to talk about.

'I took your things,' said Vee, evenly, her hands clasped under chin, her eyes on her dinner plate, 'because I wanted you to talk to me.'

'Huh?'

'That is what I mean. Please don't say 'huh', say I beg your pardon, if you have to.' She raised her eyes from her plate and looked at him, and her look was not entirely hostile.

'These things of yours, machines, toys, whatever you want to call them. They're a distraction. They're a way of hiding from the world. I am not stupid, I don't pretend to know what they are or how they work. I just know they are not real. They are a way of not being in the present. You are living in a fantasy world and you no longer know how to communicate with a human being.'

There was a bit of a pause. Jason was pushing a piece of tomato around his plate.

'Well?'

'It's none of your fucking business.'

'And you will speak to me without using profanities.'

'Why?'

'Because . . .'

'Because you say so.'

'Because that is the way the world works. People who have to live together have to have a regard for one another, respect. That is all I ask, a little respect.'

'Why should you care?'

'Because I . . .'

'You think my dad was a piece of shit.' He was speaking quietly and still pushing the tomato around his plate. 'You don't know, you didn't know him.'

'And nor . . .'

'Just because he was black. Because you're a racist.' He

was still not looking at her. 'And you have the fucking . . . to talk to me about respect.'

'I was brought up to learn . . .'

'Respect? What does it mean, eh? What do you think it means?'

'It means . . .' Vee swallowed hard. 'Respect means . . .' She paused for a moment.

'See? You don't know. Shall I tell you what respect means?' He was looking directly at her now. 'It means looking up to someone because you think they're cool, they're okay, maybe they're even better than okay. Is that right? Is that what you call respect?'

It was the longest sentence he'd ever spoken to her. And he was on a roll now.

'You!' He was making stabbing motions at her now with his fork. 'Haven't got the first fucking idea about respect. Because you think you're better than the rest of us! You think because you're old you have the right to tell us, to tell me, what to do! And what I want to know is who gave you that right? Huh?'

'I do have . . .'

'You don't know! You don't have a fucking clue! You know why? Because you're the one living in fantasy land, man! Not – a – fucking – clue! You said so yourself! You don't know – my things, you don't have the first fucking clue what they are, you just – assume there's something wrong because you don't know what they fucking are!'

And then there was silence. And Jason lowered his fork and sat with his head slumped, shaking slightly, and Vee realised he was crying.

'Oh Jason,' she said, and she reached out and laid her hand on his wrist, and this time he did not pull away.

'I am sorry for the things I said about your father,' said Vee. She was stroking his arm now. 'You are right, I didn't know him, but I did know what he did to your mother, and to you. And maybe I am . . . But it's that that makes me dislike him. Isn't that quite natural?'

His tears were dropping in great globules onto his plate.

'It was only because I care for you,' she found herself saying, and wondered as she said it if there was any truth in it.

Jason blinked and brushed roughly at his eyes.

16

Ellie arrived on the doorstep at four o'clock in the afternoon. She'd come straight from the airport.

'So?' she said to her aunt, a tad over eagerly.

'You're back,' said Vee, redundantly, before turning and hobbling off down the hallway. 'Jason!' she called. 'Your mother's here!'

There was a pause while no one appeared. Ellie wheeled her suitcase across the threshold and closed the door behind her. She was watchful. She felt her heart pounding. Ridiculous.

Jason sidled round the doorway of the living room and stared at her.

'Good trip?' he said.

'Excellent, thank you.' It wasn't true, she'd spent most of the time half out of her mind in worry, especially since her brother had confiscated her mobile. 'How about you?'

'Me?'

'Yes.'

'I haven't been anywhere.'

She laughed, nervously. She felt suddenly shy, and out of place.

'Your aunt is weird.'

'Oh! In what way, precisely?'

'She can't get the hang of chess. She thinks she can but she can't.'

'Chess? Have you been playing . . .?'

But he'd gone. She walked down the hallway to the living room. Vee was sitting at the dining table, the board in front of her. She looked up as Ellie came in and said, 'He cheats!'

'What, my son? What are you saying Aunt Vee?'

'See what I mean?' Jason sat down opposite her.

'He never . . .' Ellie's mouth was hanging open, she was aware of it but couldn't help herself. She was going to say, 'He's never played chess in his life before,' but she thought she perhaps shouldn't. She thought she should perhaps just shut up and watch.

So she did. She stood there, in the doorway, still in her coat, still holding onto her suitcase, looking on at the two most important people in her life playing chess, almost like old friends. She heaved a silent sigh of relief and, for the first time for two weeks, or maybe for much longer than that, she felt calm.

21ˢᵗ century woman (part 2)

CONSUMMATION

We met at a pub by the river,
One lunchtime somewhere in Richmond,
The sun on the water was shimmering
On that sparkling October day.
And we talked about everything under the sun
Like old friends, that's how it seemed.
And from that moment on
I was his.
Together we stood by the river,
While the rest of the world disappeared,
Me and my future lover,
On that fateful October day.
Time stood still as he kissed me,
Then he held me close and he said to me:
'I feel I've known you all my life.'
Yes, he really did say that.

Thirty-three years of living,
Twelve years of marriage,
A husband, two kids and a mortgage,
That's where I am today,
Here on the edge of a cliff

Thinking: Oh God, what am I doing?
Help me someone, before it's too late.
It's too late.

I'm a 21st century woman,
Pragmatic and single-minded,
Got a career, a suit and a laptop,
I can hold my own in a boardroom.
But I'm afraid you'll have to forgive me,
'Cause I'm not the person I was.
Though responsibility
Once meant the world to me,
Now it's gone,
Flown
Right out of the window.

I'm a 21st century woman,
Mature and independent,
Got a brain, a degree and ambition,
Always knew where I was going.
But I'm afraid you're going to despise me,
'Cause I'm not the woman I was.
Don't tell me I'm wrong,
I've been waiting so long,
I have not lived a life
Till this moment.

Prudence and Stella

This story, set in London in Victorian times, features a real and well-known (in her time) person. But while details of her life have been carefully researched this particular story is total fiction.

First love? It may surprise you, it did me. It was unrequited – isn't it always? – but it was innocent too, and wonderful, not to say unconventional, and a deal more satisfying than most of what came after.

I had an unusual upbringing. I had parents, a mother in particular, who didn't really care much what their daughter was up to, so I spent the best part of my childhood unsupervised. I am not saying I was neglected, I was simply left to my own devices, and there was never a shortage of those.

At a young age I took to wandering the streets of my neighbourhood and skinny-dipping in the ponds at Regents Park, until an unnecessarily officious member of the Metropolitan Police gave me an earful for breaking not just one but two 'by-laws', as he called them – swimming in the ponds and not wearing a bathing suit.

You could say I learned life's lessons the short way. I did exactly what I felt like doing until someone stopped me. It was one of the joys of my unrestrained youth.

My wanderings eventually took me to the West End, where I met this young lad called Mikey hanging around the stage door of the Adelphi Theatre. (Mikey is the one who stole my virginity, not my heart. I was seventeen years old and it was high time. He is not important to this particular story except in that he was responsible, since he was working behind the scenes at the theatre at the time, for my being in a position to meet my first love.) Mikey did not introduce us, I did that all on my own.

The first time I set eyes on her I was sitting idly in the auditorium watching the stage crew at work when this tall, willowy creature in a straw hat appeared at the side of the stage and stood there for several minutes while nobody took the slightest notice. Eventually a man in shirtsleeves came over to her and they had what looked to me to be an altercation, though I couldn't hear a word they were saying over the banging and crashing of the carpenter. After a few minutes, during which she became increasingly agitated, she stormed off the stage in what might have been tears.

The next time I saw her she was on the stage, in costume, performing. Mikey managed to sneak me into a performance through the pass door but not until after the second half, so I had very little idea what was going on.

I'll tell you here and now I'm not one for the theatre. It's frankly senseless, in my view, to pay a heap of money to watch actors in ludicrous clothes and too much makeup walking out on a stage and talking in a loud voice to nobody in particular. It's too artificial for words. But what struck me on that occasion, and I use the word advisedly, was the transformation. It took me some time to realise that the utterly gorgeous creature standing centre-stage beneath the lights was the same frail-looking thing I had seen hovering at the side of the stage days before. In the midst of all the eye-popping and the bellowing at the audience in order, so I understand, to be seen and heard by the folk in the gallery, there was this . . . miracle. There was no other word for her.

I believe I startled the rest of the audience by leaping to my feet at the curtain call and shouting 'Bravo!', because that was not what was done in the theatre back in the 1890s, not even at the Adelphi. Needless to say it wasn't the play I was applauding as I never did catch on to what it was all about and nor did I care as it seemed too silly for words.

I didn't think twice about presenting myself right away at her dressing room door, tapping loudly and hearing her call out 'Come'.

She was sitting at her dressing table gazing blankly at the mirror. She was still dressed in her stage clothes, a skimpy black number that accentuated her frailness, and her still made-up face in the reflection of the harsh lights made her look quite unearthly. I wanted to touch her to see if she was real, but instead I stood behind her chair for some time before she appeared to notice me. At which point, without really looking at me, she said, 'Do I know you?'

'No,' I said. 'My name's Prudence.'

There was a small pause before she smiled slightly and said, 'And are you?'

I ignored this. I'd heard every joke there was to hear about my name. I just said – blurted rather – 'I wanted to tell you I think you are wonderful.' It sounded ridiculous then and it sounds even more ridiculous now, but it was truly meant.

She looked at me briefly and away again. 'Thank you, darling,' she said. It was the first time anyone had called me darling and it made my heart almost leap right out of its socket. 'I'm glad someone thinks so.'

She then pulled at a wad of cotton wool, tore open the

lid of a large tub of cream and proceeded to smear the stuff over her face. She rubbed at it with such violence it was as if she was trying to obliterate herself.

'I hope you're not thinking of entering this profession darling because if you are, think again.' She snatched at another dollop of cream and scrubbed away at her lips. 'They are nothing other than charlatans and back-stabbers, it's a profession fit only for mad people.'

When I didn't immediately reply she swivelled in her chair and looked right at me. The makeup around her eyes, smeared by the cream, made her look like something you might meet on a dark night at Hallowe'en.

'Then why did you choose it?' I ventured, quite bravely in the circumstances.

It was an obvious question but it seemed to take her by surprise. She swivelled back to face the mirror and said, savagely, 'I was given the sack today. They told me my performance is below par, I have a 'weak voice' and 'feeble gestures'. Two weeks' notice. And all because of their execrable play, and the abominable notices. I am the scapegoat.'

'So what are you going to do?'

She stared at my reflection. 'Kill myself maybe.'

'Oh! But you can't – you mustn't!'

She laughed. 'I am not serious. Well, not really.'

By now the makeup was gone and there was her face, naked and shiny, and I felt at that moment an overwhelming feeling of protectiveness. I wanted to wrap her in my arms and hold her to me. This woman, this girl – she could not have been more than a few years older than me – this unearthly creature, opening herself up to a complete stranger. Oh, glorious!

'Perhaps I can help you,' I found myself saying.

'Help me? How?'

'I could be your assistant, or your dresser.'

She got up from her chair and went to a corner of the room and proceeded to remove her costume. There was no self-consciousness, it was as if I was her oldest and most intimate friend.

'I couldn't afford to pay you, darling. Anyway, there's nothing to assist me with, let alone dress me in, if I'm out of work.'

She stood stock still for a moment, in the shadows, in her undergarments. She looked like a small, lonely, vulnerable child.

'You won't be out of work for long. I guarantee it.'

One does say the stupidest things when one is young. But to her credit, she just smiled and, as she pulled her dress down from its hanger she looked at me and said, 'What a strange creature you are. Where did you spring from?'

I was about to tell her about Mikey but quickly realised she was not looking for a literal answer.

'You dear thing,' she said. 'Dear, odd looking thing. Hook me up, would you?'

So I did, with trembling fingers, fumbling, her body so close to me I could barely breathe.

She spoke more softly then. 'I do it for my children,' she said, 'and for my mother and for my husband. So that we all may eat.'

'You're married?' I tried and failed to keep the panic from my voice. I don't know what I was thinking really, or expecting; but hooks done, she turned around and gave me a pat on the cheek.

'He's a long way away, in Africa, I've not seen him for six years. His health is even worse than mine and he struggles, more than me even.' She gave me a wan smile.

'Do you love him?' I cried. I was fighting for breath.

'Oh yes,' she said gently. 'Passionately.'

She laughed out loud then and before I knew what she

was doing she drew me to her and gave me a hug. It was the first hug I had ever received in my life, and as hugs go it was not effusive. It was more like hugging an object than a person, she was so boned and corseted. And the hug said, which she did not, 'Don't be disappointed.' And it was over.

~

To cut a longish story short, I went on to become Stella's dresser. Yes, we were on first-name terms in no time, partly due to my refusal to call her by the name she was popularly known as, which was Mrs Patrick Campbell. (Why? – I asked myself, when her husband had nothing to do with her success, quite the opposite, he didn't even live in the same country.) You've heard of her, of course you have, even if you can't quite place her. Despite these rough beginnings – the management changed their minds about sacking her when she had another offer from another theatre – she went on to become a big star of the theatre well into the twentieth century. Famous playwrights such as Mr Pinero and Mr Shaw wrote plays especially for her.

We became friends and confidants. We helped one another through our respective trials and tribulations and cried on one another's shoulders when we needed to. It helped of course that I was not and never pretended to be her rival when it came to looks, not to mention the acting or the ambition. She tried her best to groom me, to make me look at least respectable enough to be seen on special occasions out on the town with her. Or if not with her exactly, part of her *entourage*, following in her wake like a satellite, along with her publicist, agent, hairstylist and a number of other hangers-on. There was a time when she was being introduced to royalty – Queen Alexandra as I recall – and as she curtseyed to the ground she caught my eye and I swear she winked at me.

Of course we lost touch over the years. She became too

busy for the likes of little me, though she did come to my wedding.

Friends scoffed, and called it hero worship, or lesbian attraction, and I say so what, call it what you like, I don't care. It was real enough then, and uncomplicated, and natural, and all-round glorious. It was my first love and it came without baggage, and nothing else that arrived in my later life could match it. (Except Fred of course. But that's another story.)

The full story of Prudence's remarkable life can be found in my novel 'The Purpose of Prudence de Vere'.

A state of grace

When I was twelve years old my parents sent me to a high church Anglican girls' school, where we went to chapel twice a day and the services were conducted in Latin. I've no idea why they chose this particular school; as agnostics themselves it was certainly not for the purpose of the religious instruction.

Academically I learned very little, education being quite low on the list of school priorities which, roughly speaking, went: God, order, discipline, God, obedience, quiet, no-talking-after-lights-out and, if there was time and energy left, passing the odd exam. We never studied or discussed the Bible and we were never taught the meaning of parable and allegory; and since hymns and prayers were performed in Latin we only ever had the haziest idea of what they were all about. Being a pliant child this didn't bother me. I never questioned anything.

The highlight of the school year was the Nativity Play, held in the local church in December, parents invited, at which I was granted two years in a row – which was unprecedented – what to me was the highest honour of all: to deliver the final Lesson. I was tutored by the headmistress, who'd been a professional actress in her youth. Again we did not discuss the meaning of the words, we did not in fact *discuss* anything. She instructed me, syllable by syllable, on intonation, pitch, emphasis and rhythm. In particular, rythm.

> *In the beginning* (beat) *was the Word.*
> *And the Word was with God.*
> *And the Word* (beat) *was God.*
> *The same was in the beginning with God,*
> *All things were made by Him.*
> *Without Him was not anything made that was made.*

We went over it, syllable by syllable, again and again. She had me repeating each phrase after her, copying her precisely – *The same was in the beginning <u>with</u> God* – and while it shames me now to admit it I Ioved every minute of it. I loved her precision, her persistence, and above all I loved it when at long last she nodded and quietly said, 'That's it'.

At fifteen I was confirmed, which involved going to Confession, for the first and last time in my life, after which I spent a Quiet Week of contemplation, away from all worldly things including homework. I confessed to the mortal sin of self-righteousness – it was the best I could come up with – after which having been exonerated I felt more self-righteous than ever. In the week that followed I experienced such peace, harmony and love I began to understand what it was to be in a state of grace.

I had fallen in love with God. I had not the faintest idea who He was or who decided He was who He was. I never questioned what the Bible really meant, nor who had written it, nor did I care. I was possessed with feelings of such immense power I almost levitated.

It didn't last of course. I emerged from the holy powerhouse a clueless, high-minded little prig and completely unprepared for the outside world. When I began to realise how tenuous was my understanding of real life and the way things worked I started to doubt the object of my love. I even questioned the meaning of the Lesson I had been so proud to deliver two years in a row. *In the beginning was the Word.* What did it mean? How could there be a Word with no one to say it? And what Word was it anyway, precisely? And so on. I switched from piety to atheism in the flick of an eye. Lacking something I joined the Humanist Society and attended lectures by Freddie Ayer. But it didn't do it for me. Eventually I settled somewhere in between, right there on the rational, agnostic fence, an unbeliever who really wanted to believe but couldn't find the evidence to justify it.

And so I lived my life, in an unplanned, unreligious and sometimes chaotic fashion. There were good times and bad times but I could find no real purpose in anything in particular. I was a disenchanted agnostic.

And now here I am in the Cathedral attending a carol service – the only time in years I've been near a church, and even now I can't quite bring myself to join in the prayers. I see the Cross, processing, held high above the heads of the congregation, I feel the sense of pomp, marvel at the richness of the clergy in their black and red, listen moist-eyed to the unaccompanied choirboy singing *Once in Royal David's City* at the far end of the nave. I leap at the sudden blast of the organ and smile at the idiosyncrasy of the sound system which makes us all turn to stare at the speakers attached to the walls rather than the real-life speakers at the pulpit. Then comes climax of the service:

In the beginning was the Word

It's the same version as the one I knew so well. It makes no more sense now than it ever did, but it doesn't matter, not in the least.

The Canon tells a joke about Mick Jagger, then preaches about love, in that vague, churchy, John-Lennony kind of a way. He knows a good proportion of the congregation are there, like me, as a once-a-year experience. *Love.* What is that? Do I love the friend I am sitting next to? Do I love the neighbour on my other side who I've never met before? *Love.* Who, or what, or why? Would it make an atom's difference to anything in this world if we loved? Would wars cease if we loved? If it's so easy why don't we all just do it? *Love.*

I've no idea. All I know is for a fleeting moment, for the length of the service and perhaps for a short while afterwards, I find myself right back where I was all those years ago: in a state of grace.

Vera Simmonds

The first thing he remembered Miss Simmonds saying to him was 'Aren't you a bit young to be going to school alone?' Which annoyed him no end and to which he replied:

'I'm not alone, I've got Larry with me.'

'Larry?' said Miss Simmonds, smiling. 'Who's Larry?'

'Larry,' he said, with emphasis, as if to a stupid person. His eyes flicked sideways and Miss Simmonds, after a moment's hesitation, threw back her head and laughed. 'Larry, I see. And how are you Larry?'

He had only recently taken to visiting the corner shop on his way to school, and not every day, because it was not every day he could afford the bag of crisps, which is all he ever bought. It didn't take long before Miss Simmonds began to greet him as an old friend, he and Larry too. There were other times too, when he was sent to the shop to buy stuff like bread and milk and the odd packet of fish fingers. In time he got chatting with Miss Simmonds, he even allowed a bit of extra time on his way to school to allow for it. One day she asked him, on an off-the-cuff kind of a way, whether the bag of crisps was all he had to eat for lunch, at which he shrugged. From then on she slipped something extra into the bag – an apple perhaps, and in time a cheese sandwich, and then maybe another apple 'for Larry'. She never mentioned it, he never mentioned it, she certainly didn't charge him for any of it.

She asked him to call her Vera, which was her first name, she told him. They laughed about names. He was Leo the lion and Larry was Larry the lamb, he said. 'And do you live up to your names?' she asked, twinkling at him from behind her glasses. He didn't really understand the question, so he just laughed instead.

Nowadays a mother like Leo's would have been placed into the hands of social services, and he, Leo, would probably have been taken into care, and the school would definitely have been alerted. As it was his mum spent her days lying on the sofa, popping pills and sleeping a lot. She rarely went out. She never asked him about school, or about anything else. Leo didn't question this, why would he? He was her carer, her housekeeper, her shopper, it was all a perfectly natural part of his life.

So it was grand to make a friend of Vera Simmonds. He knew he could talk to her about anything and she was always interested, and never judged him. Unlike Larry, who as time went on and his friendship with Vera deepened became a less essential part of his life, she was always happy to discuss things with him, light-heartedly, always with that twinkle in her eye. Nothing seemed to faze her. He told her things he would never tell his mum. Detention, for not doing his homework. Coming bottom in the class, because he did not pay attention. 'Oh my,' she would sigh. 'It brings it all back to me. School days. Well I'll tell you something for nothing Leo, I was terrible at school. I was bottom of the class too. And now look at me! I'm a successful businesswoman. I've been running this place for nigh on – what – thirty years now. It doesn't make me rich, but it certainly makes me happy. And that's all that matters in the end, isn't it?'

There was one occasion when he was coming home

from school, later than usual because of detention, and he bumped into Vera outside her shop. She was just shutting up. 'Early today,' she said, it being Thursday or something. Then she said, 'Do you fancy a bit of a walk? It's a lovely afternoon.'

He hesitated, and then he agreed, and so together they wandered off down the street to the park. He hadn't been to the park for ages, there didn't seem to be any point. As parks go it was no great shakes. A playground, a sort of pond, some trees, and a café. But with Vera by his side it was altogether different.

She told him about the day the park opened, twenty years or so ago, and some visiting dignitary – 'A mayor or someone' – who she didn't believe had set foot in the village before, made a long and boring speech about how wonderful it was and how it would transform the place. She then went to tell him the names of all the ducks – there was a good variety of those, for some reason. To Leo they were ducks, but Vera seemed to know the names of all the different breeds, and where they came from, and why they chose to stay put in this unprepossessing pond. 'Because they get fed, basically,' she said. She pointed out the differences between the coots – 'With the white noses, aggressive buggers, excuse my French' – and the milder-mannered moorhens. He was more impressed by the swearing than by the birds themselves. Then she went on to describe the trees – you could tell what they were from the bark, or from the leaves of course, when there were any. Again, to Leo they were all just trees, some smaller than others maybe, but just trees nonetheless. She told him how and why some of them lost their leaves in winter and others didn't. He'd heard it all before of course, in biology class, but like most things in class he hadn't been paying attention.

As they left the park they passed by a small group of

Leo's fellow schoolboys. He nodded at them and as they walked on he heard them burst into laughter. 'Don't mind them,' said Vera.

'What were you doing with old Miss Boggle-Eyes?' they jeered at him the next day. It was in the school playground, and they seemed to be surrounding. He wished Larry had been there for moral support.

'What do you mean, "Boggle-Eyes"?'

'Boggle Eyes. She boggles at you,' said one.

'Her glasses are like bottles,' said another.

'Bottle eyes!' said another, and they hooted with laughter.

'She's a witch,' said one of them.

And so on and so on.

It was harmless enough, in itself. But it got Leo wondering.

If you'd asked him at any point what Vera Simmonds looked like he'd have been hard pressed to describe her. But now they'd said all of that, his schoolmates, he began to look at her a bit more closely. It's true her glasses were thick, so thick that when you looked directly at her through them her eyes seemed all lopsided and wobbly. And there was a wart on her right cheek, close to her mouth, and he had heard somewhere that this was the sign of a witch. Only witches had warts. He began to feel a little self-conscious.

The last time he saw her was on a Thursday afternoon when she shut up shop early. Their Thursday afternoon walks had become a bit of a fixture by now. Sometimes they strolled through the park, sometimes they walked down to the river, or just wandered the streets. She talked to him nonstop during these walks, commonplace stuff mostly, about her life, her childhood, being brought up in this village and how it used to be way back when. She never mentioned a husband or kids, he assumed there weren't any.

She rarely asked about his home life but when he did open up about a mother who spent her waking life half asleep she listened, and nodded, but never commented. She related colourful anecdotes about some of the weirder characters who once lived in the village. Of Fred Mason, the postman, who liked to drink a bit and who more than once fell into the river on his way home of an evening and had to be fished out by a passer-by. (There always was a passer-by it seemed.) Of Mrs Carbuncle, so-called – not her real name but it was what everyone called her – who people had down as a witch because she was so often seen wandering into the woods at night-time and only emerging in the morning. And one day as they were passing by the huge and ancient wall that enclosed the local manor she told him about Sir Wordry Willforth – 'how's that for a name, eh? – who once owned the entire village back in the old days and who, so the story goes, used to own a smuggling ring and one day ran off with the housekeeper's daughter. How many of these tales were true Leo could only guess, but it didn't matter. Vera brought what he had already thought of as a sleepy village that one day he would be shot of and never visit again, truly alive.

The jeers at school continued, on and off, but it was enough. So eventually Leo took a diversion on his way to school via another corner shop. It added a good ten minutes onto his journey and the new place did not provide him with a cheery smile and a free lunch. In fact there was virtually no interaction between Leo and the grim-faced man behind the counter at all. And that was just what Leo wanted.

~

And now here he is, several decades on and far away from the village of his birth and upbringing, and somebody –

Leo wasn't sure who, but guessed it was someone from his old school – has sent him an obituary of Vera Simmonds, who has died aged ninety. Ninety. That means she would have been fifty when he befriended her, hardly the old woman of his childhood memory, and barely ten years older than he is now. She had continued to work into her eighties, it said, and she had died alone. Nobody seemed to know of any surviving family members. The funeral took place last Friday.

She had died alone, with no family members attending the funeral.

She had had one child, but nobody was to know that. He was not her child, but she was the nearest the child had had to a mother. A mother who now he came to think of it, in his middle-aged maturity, he had loved more than his biological mother, who was only a very distant memory. He could see her now, Vera Simmonds, a dumpy, lumpy little woman with no grace and very little beauty other than those extraordinary eyes, magnified and distorted through the bottle-bottomed lens of her glasses, that looked out at the world with wonder and merriment; a woman who truth be told had gleaned more sheer delight from the limited surroundings of a small village in Shropshire than he, Leo, had gained through years of global travel.

He had missed her funeral. And perhaps most importantly, he had missed her old age. Her lonely old age, which just might have been enlivened by grandchildren, his own, grandmother-less children; whose lives would – he had no doubt at all – have been enlivened by her beyond possible measure.

The old couple

You couldn't help noticing the old couple in the supermarket. To begin with they were always there, and always bickering. It was a quiet bickering, so quiet that even when you were standing right by them – pretending to study the labels on the cartons of fruit juice, or canned beans, so as not to draw attention to your eavesdropping – you could barely make out what they were saying. On one occasion they were hovering around the booze department, he with a bottle of whisky in one hand, poised halfway between shelf and trolley, she quietly haranguing him about something or other. And you'd think – how sad is that, to get to that age and not be able to afford the odd bottle of whisky? Or worse, to be living with someone who disapproved of your drinking? After all, what else is there when you get to that age?

After you'd come across them two or three times you caught her eye, and you said 'Hello' as brightly as anything, and she'd just stare back as if she'd never seen you in her life before. Which of course she hadn't. You may have been watching their every move but she didn't know you from Eve. Besides, this is London, and nobody talks to strangers in a supermarket in London.

By now you're building up quite a picture about them. You can tell a lot about someone from their shopping habits. For a start they used a trolley even though they bought hardly anything. They didn't have a car, you knew that because you saw them walking off down the road with their bags. So that's why they were in there *every day*, just buying enough for that one day. You couldn't help peering in when you were behind them in the checkout queue – a half pint of skimmed milk, a carton of eggs, a loaf of sliced bread (brown, not multi-grain), some chicken pieces (not free-range) and a bag of spinach, a couple of potatoes, and that was it. And when they got to the till they do what all old people do – they pay in vouchers, and pennies, which she has spread in the palm of her hand, and it takes two of them, her and the person at the till, to count them out one by one, all the time laughing and chatting away to each other as if they were the only the people in the entire place; while you're standing there invisible, shifting from one foot to the other, trying not to sigh, trying not to look at your phone for the umpteenth time, trying not to kill them.

After a while you begin to resent them. After all old people have all day to shop, so why do they want to go clogging up the aisles when the place is at its busiest with you and all those other people like you – working people that is – stocking up on your way home from work?

One day you find yourself following them home. Well not quite home, and not deliberately, not as in *stalking*, more out of idle curiosity. And you're surprised to realise they live quite a way away, and up quite a steep hill. And you're even more surprised to see him take her arm, as she's struggling a bit.

Old age is freaky. Living from one hospital appointment to another, what's the point? Not to mention what they're costing you – you the younger generation, paying for their pensions out of your tax, no way anyone under pension age could afford to buy a property – not that you necessarily want to buy a property, but all the same.

It gets you thinking about your own parents who after all are not that much younger than them, in their early sixties. They bickered too, or so you assumed. They separated when you were too young to realise that's not what everyone does. Divorce, that is, not bicker.

For a while you don't see the old couple. They are significant by their absence, you could say, and against your better judgment you start to worry about them. Have they finally popped their clogs? If not both of them, then one or the other? It would be silly to say you miss them, you miss them like you miss a bad cold, but you can't help looking around for them every time you enter the shop. You think about asking someone, the manager or the person behind the till, but you'd feel an idiot not even knowing their names.

And then one day just as you'd forgotten all about them, there they are again. Only he is in a wheelchair and he has a tube up his nose and she is wheeling him clumsily around the aisles, missing the shelves by a whisker, shunting back and forth back and forth every time they try to turn a corner, and giggling. You watch them heading away up the street and you wonder how she's going to manage that hill with him in a wheelchair, bearing in mind the trouble she had when she was on her own two feet. You think about going after them and offering to help. But somehow you don't. You're afraid it might be intrusive, or none of your business – there's no end of reasons why people don't offer to do these things.

The next time it's late summer at a street party organised for the local community, and there they are, and to your surprise he's up on his feet again. No tubes, no wheelchairs. At one point there is music playing and a few people begin to dance, and blow me down but they're joining in in a kind of ballroom dancing way, swaying their hips this way and that and making everyone around them laugh, and then begin to clap, in rhythm, and in no time they're the centre of attention and they're looking at one another and laughing their heads off. It's at that point you begin to wonder if you had it all wrong. If the bickering couple you thought just tolerated one another actually were . . . how can you say this? Looking after one another. Bickering still, no doubt, but then all couples bicker, don't they? And these two, with all the things that are wrong with them, but still together, still able to enjoy things together. Which let's face it is more than you've managed to do in your own short life.

Who knows what goes on behind closed doors? In the end they have each other. And that has to be worth something, doesn't it?

Maybe old age isn't as bad as it's cracked up to be.

Colleen and me

Breaking news: 'The body of Colleen Leonard was found early this morning on Hampstead Heath. Police are investigating.'

Colleen and me go way back, to early secondary school. We were like that (I'm crossing fingers). People used to say we were a weird pair since she was so pretty and I was so, well, not. But then other people said it wasn't so weird, pretty people often like to hang out with plain friends because it makes them look good, and there's no competition. They used to call me her gofer, her acolyte – I had to look that one up – which wasn't the case as it happens, it maybe just looked that way. They even asked me if I was envious of her and I said no way, because what they didn't realise is how dependent she was and how, well, helpless, used to people doing things for her and stuff. Like choosing places to go at night and films to see and holidays even, and organising it all, which is what I'm good at.

When she hit the big time, which she did in her GCSE year – she was discovered, in a club, by a model agency. Actually she'd been 'discovered' several times before that, just walking down the street, and some of them were highly dodgy as you can imagine. But this time it was for real, and they asked her to come in and do a photo shoot and it just took off from there. So she left school before her As and I did too as it was sort of assumed that I'd be the one looking after her, you know, making sure everything was okay.

My parents threw a blue fit at me leaving before sixth form but I told them, this is the chance of a lifetime and you know what, if I'm not around to look after Coll then two things will happen. I'll have missed the opportunity of a lifetime, and she'll be left out there on her own, prey for the first shark that comes along, and there were plenty of those, believe me.

It was like air traffic control, what with accountants and lawyers and publicists and stylists, handling all of them and protecting Collie from the press – believe me if the world's tabloids had sent all their reporters along at the same time they would never have laid hands on Coll's phone number, not on my watch. And people kept on asking me if I was jealous and I'd say, you know what, I wouldn't be Coll for quids. She's had it all so easy you see, everything has just landed on her lap – except for her parents of course, but they didn't really feature in her life one way or another. And the world isn't doing anyone a favour by making things that easy as it's the hard knocks that make a person who they are, in my view. Coll had no hard knocks at all so she had no survival techniques because she didn't actually need them. Who would want to be that vulnerable?

I actually got propositioned myself, more than once in fact. I wasn't fooled, I knew they weren't interested in Flat-Faced Jane (it's what people called me even though my name is actually Lilian, though I do have a flat face I suppose), they just wanted to snuggle up to me so they could get their dirty hands on Coll's number. But I didn't mind one bit because frankly, if it hadn't been for her no one would have given me a second glance as it's not as if I have a sparkling personality or anything, and one or two of them turned out to be quite nice and we had a bit of a thing, not serious, but fun anyway.

Then when the film people came along and said they wanted Coll in one of their movies I said to Coll – Don't. Really, don't do it. You're a model and you are very beautiful and all but you're not an actress. You never acted in your life. It's a different thing altogether, you'll make a grand fool of yourself. But she was insistent. Or rather they were insistent, offering her so much money it made my eyes water. In the end of course she said yes and we all know what happened next, well, you'd think she'd be destroyed, the things they said about her, but she really wasn't. She just said well everyone has to start somewhere and laughed and said they'd offered her another part in another film and she was going to go for it and this time she was going to have acting classes and she was going to *show them.*

Then we had a falling out. I guess by this time I'd become her sort of minder, protecting her not just from the press but from Doubtful People, the sort who Do Drugs and generally waste their lives away. She had no idea, she was so nice to everyone and she couldn't see when they were taking advantage – and I don't just mean sexually – she was a naturally nice person, despite everything. I don't mean a person can't be beautiful and a nice person at the same time but if you really have everything on a plate and people running around you telling you you're *amazing, awesome, super-talented,* and doing everything for you then it's quite easy to turn a bit you-know-what. But she didn't, and she wasn't, she just kept on loving everyone.

So anyway I walked away from her for a month, went on holiday and didn't give her a thought. And of course as soon as I came back I could see she'd started on the rocky road. I went through her place with a fine-toothed comb and threw out everything she could swallow or smoke or stuff up her nose, and that included what she claimed were vitamin pills – so why were they in an unmarked box? – and packets of flour – as what was someone who never cooked in her life doing with flour in her store cupboard? I thought she'd see red, she'd shout and tell me to get the hell out of her life but she didn't, she just cried and hugged me and said please Lil, sleep with me tonight. And no she didn't mean it that way she meant literally please sleep with me tonight, so I did, and we had a girly cuddle and she calmed down and slept like a baby, as did I as it happens.

I thought then, actually you know what, she is quite something, is Colleen Leonard. She is not just a beautiful face, and a lovely person, this girl has got guts. Yes. Guts. If you've never had the press all over you one minute and digging in the knife the next, then you've no idea what that girl went through. I tried to protect her from the worst of it but short of shutting her up in a cage and confiscating her phone, well. She just picked herself up and did the acting classes and between you and me they didn't make a spot of difference, but the next film wasn't half so bad, she was actually quite good, even the press thought so, some of them. But the funny thing was, well I could never compete with her on the looks front, never wanted to, but when it came to something like acting, I wasn't so sure. People never asked me if I envied her film career but actually you know what, I sort of did.

Trouble was the more she had to do with the film business the more Dodgy People she got involved with, and they didn't like me at all, not surprisingly. They called me the Nazi, and all because I was trying to protect her from herself. I caught her out one morning lying on her bed glassy-eyed and I said for Christ's sake Coll *what are you doing?* and she looked at me as if she hadn't the faintest idea who I was. So I told her I can't keep going through all your things with the fine-toothed comb and she said well who asked you to do that in the first place? She got quite shirty. And the next thing was she changed the locks, and soon after that she sacked me.

It wasn't her that sacked me, I always knew that, it was the Company she Kept, you know those film types who claim they can't get out of bed until they've had a snort and how it enhances their creativity and all that and I'm thinking, give us a break, she was fine until you came along. And she was, really, she didn't need that stuff, whatever it is that makes some people turn to drugs, she didn't have that. I used to say to her life is difficult enough without having to cope with drug dependency and she used to laugh and say you can say that again.

I could cry. Well to be truthful I did cry. Not for myself, but for Coll. Not returning my phone calls or emails, some heavy answering her front door and telling me to get lost, and I knew it had nothing to do with her. A girl like Coll would never treat her oldest friend like that. I was beside myself. Looking back it was ironic really because it was me who put all those safeguards in place to protect her from the press and now they were protecting her from me. I had to check Twitter and the Metro to see what she was up to, and it wasn't nice. I don't know how much they were making up about her but whatever it was, it was getting out of hand, and my poor darling sweet-natured beautiful friend, well, she was turning into a witch. Photos of her in the press pouring out of nightclubs high as a kite, not my Colleen, not the Colleen I used to know. Having dinner with drooling, fat, middle-aged film producers, I mean *please*. She was turning into a cliché, and I think it's that that did it for me more than anything. Cinderella had turned into an ugly sister, well not ugly but you know what I'm trying to say. Just like all the rest. And she wasn't like that, she never used to be like that, a beautiful young woman whose life was ruined by drugs.

I knew if I could just get to see her everything'd be okay. Not right away maybe, but at least if I could just speak to her. Fortunately there was a way, something nobody could have known about and, well, last night she managed to give her minders the slip and you know what happened next.

I guess I've given the game away in a sense. And now the news is out that she's been found dead on Hampstead Heath and everyone knew about her drug habit of course they'll be jumping to obvious conclusions. But the fact is they are wrong and they'll find out sooner or later how wrong they are, which will be a good thing because otherwise they'd turn her into the ultimate cliché, I can just see the headlines: "Star of *Chinese Whispers* (that was the latest film, the one she wasn't too bad in) found dead from an overdose on Hampstead Heath". And she'd go down in history as yet another sad beautiful person who couldn't cope with her beauty and her fame and all that crap, and I couldn't bear that.

But it won't happen, because I know they're on their way, right now, as we speak. I couldn't just sit by and let it happen you see, I couldn't watch the girl I loved so much going down that slippery path because I knew that sooner or later she would end up dead from an overdose of something. And I couldn't bear to just sit back and let that happen.

Send in the clowns

Her knees were a bit troublesome these days, and she got puffed easily, especially on hills. There were slopes on streets that never used to be there. Her blood pressure went a bit crazy now and again, for no apparent reason, but she didn't let that worry her. All in all she felt she was doing pretty well for a 72-year-old.

She had not led a particularly remarkable life, not to outward appearances anyway, though when she looked back over it it seemed eventful enough. She had had one long-lasting marriage and three much-loved and now fiercely self-reliant children. She had dipped her toe into a number of different enterprises – graphic design, interior decoration and sculpture to name a few – but never really made her mark at any of them. Yet here she was, divorced, but solvent and still healthy, with a roof over her head etc etc.

It was all good.

The marriage had lasted over thirty years, which was a cause for celebration in itself. There had been very little rancour, or unkindness. There hadn't been much in the way of passion either, after that initial burst. What there had been was more of a companionship and intellectual compatibility, which are not to be sneezed at in the scheme of things. Marriage, living with someone else, had brought her less than she hoped but taught her more than she realised. It had revealed a new side to her, a measured, mature, above all *sensible* side. It was one of many examples of real life confounding expectations. When it ended, which it did by mutual consent, it went with a fizzle rather than a bang. Low key and verging on the mundane. Much as her marriage had been in a sense.

And now.

She lived on her own, in a flat she'd bought with the proceeds of the divided house. She'd never bought her own property before, it was on the whole easier than she'd expected. That was another thing: when you're doing something on your own what may seem like an insurmountable challenge is far more manageable when you know you only have yourself to rely on. 'Did you call the solicitor?' 'No, did you?' does not occur when you're on your own.

She does not regard herself as retired. She dabbles, or rather she 'works', making miniature clay figures of classic sculptures, and designing cards. She does it because she enjoys it, not to earn a living or to advance her career. She has a website to advertise her artworks, which she created herself, and she's very keen on social media. It keeps her in touch with the world. Now and again she will sell something, which justifies her view of herself as a self-employed professional who fills in a tax return every year.

She is comfortable, but not too much so. Apart from her modest earnings she lives on savings and a pension that just about cover her outgoings, which are minimal, and helped tremendously by her Freedom Pass, and by on occasion letting out her spare room. Such interesting lodgers she hosts. And how healthy it is having to occasionally make way for someone else in her home, to not get too upset about someone else using *her* mug and sitting in *her* chair; which she didn't realise were her mug or her chair until someone else dared to make use of them.

She has enough friends to keep her from getting too crotchety, or paranoid, she goes out once or even twice a week in the evenings, to a concert or a film or the theatre, sometimes with a friend and sometimes on her own, which she doesn't mind in the least. She visits galleries and art events she discovers mostly on Twitter and she watches the news assiduously. She checks the TV schedules in the *Guardian Guide* every Saturday and marks the programmes she will watch and others she will record. She has yet to discover Netflix. She downs work tools at 7pm every evening for the Channel 4 news and a glass of wine, followed by dinner in front of the television watching whatever is on at 9pm, or something she has recorded. The news makes her miserable, but she has to keep up to speed on disasters global and local because, bizarrely perhaps, it makes her feel she's doing her bit. If the phone rings and disturbs a TV show she's particularly absorbed in she doesn't answer it.

She tried internet dating, briefly, but gave up when she realised the chances of meeting someone of a suitable age who was fit enough to do things and bright enough to hold a conversation were probably unlikely. Besides, the prospect of building a relationship from scratch, at her age, is too daunting for words. She would rather spend time with her female friends.

She is content. She has cracked it. She has achieved acceptance.

~

If it had been a more engrossing programme she was watching at the time she may well have ignored the phone call. She was trying to get her head around *Luther*, which her friends said was a must-see, but despite the obvious appeal of its male star she was struggling to make sense of who was who and what the hell was going on, not helped by the fact that the bulk of it was so under-lit that on her ancient television all she could see were vague shadows shimmying across a dark grey screen.

Nonetheless she hesitated long enough before picking up the phone for the answer machine to kick in, which meant the ensuing conversation was recorded and she was able subsequently to play it back, from start to finish, *ad infinitum*, analysing every word, every syllable of every word, every intonation, pause, laugh, and anything else in between.

The conversation went like this:

'Hello?'

'Hello there, Hanny.'

There was only one person in the world who had ever called her Hanny. Nonetheless:

'Who is this?'

'Take a guess.'

After a pause: 'Hello Rory.'

'Got it in one. How are you?'

'I'm fine. Yes, okay. You?'

'What are you doing?'

'Er . . . In what sense?'

'Like right now.'

'Er . . . Nnn . . .'

'Come and have a drink with me.'

'Right now? No. Sorry, but no. I can't.'

'That's a shame.'

'You're in London?'

'For the week. So if not now, how about tomorrow?' Pause. 'Next day? Day after?'

Longer pause.

'You still there, Hanny?'

It was an absolutely outrageous thing to do, after . . . how long was it?

'Well actually I'm . . . I'm about to go away as it

happens.'

What was she saying?

'Where are you going?'

'Well – nowhere. Just to see friends. Sort of.' A pause. She heard him sigh. 'Okay then. The day after tomorrow?'

'Day after tomorrow's good. La Rosalita in Mount Street, do you know it?'

'I can find it.'

'Seven thirty?'

'Seven thirty is fine.'

'I look forward to it Hanny.'

'Me too.'

'Lots to catch up on. *Lots* to catch up on.'

Click.

She stood stock still for nearly a minute. She realised she'd forgotten to breathe, so she took one deep breath, and then another, until she felt her heart rate return to normal.

Just because you hold someone in your head for some years doesn't mean they do likewise. She listened to the message again, this time looking for something in the tone of the voice to indicate an intention, a motivation. He sounded casual, unchanged, no sign of nervousness or apprehension. Assertive, certainly, confident definitely. Eager?

The following morning she booked an appointment to have her hair highlighted. She'd been meaning to do it for some time but couldn't justify the expense. She emerged looking much as she'd looked before she went in, albeit seventy quid more glamorous.

She caught the tube to John Lewis in Oxford Street to buy a new outfit. It took her quite a while and several trips to the fitting room. It was so long since she'd bought anything from anywhere other than a charity shop or a market she'd forgotten what her taste was. She settled on something with a touch of sparkle and just the far side of *risqué;* but when it came to it she chickened out and wore an old favourite, since she preferred comfort to glamour and she did not want to look as if she was *trying too hard.*

There were delays on the underground on her way into town, due, according to the driver's tetchy announcement, to 'certain persons surfing the train'. This was not a pastime she'd come across before, but as the train stopped dead at Finchley Road station for what seemed like ten minutes she found herself heaving sighs of relief. With a bit of luck she'd be so late he wouldn't wait for her and she could just turn around and . . .

She was five minutes late, and he was still there.

~

The following morning Hannah's neighbour across the road, whose name she could never remember but who described herself as a one-woman neighbourhood watch, was gazing through her window as Hannah turned up at her front door at 10am with a silly grin on her face. She wasn't necessarily aware of the grin until she saw her neighbour looking at her, at which she gave a little wave and turned away to hide her blush. The same thing happened the following day. The morning after that Hannah did not appear at all. The next day she arrived at much the same time, this time sporting what her neighbour could see was a sparkly number underneath her coat. This time the silly grin was gone.

Inside her flat Hannah sat down on the sofa, still in her coat, and contemplated.

She was trying to process the last few days.

She was a mature – no, an elderly – self-sufficient woman. She had reached what she considered to be the nearest she could get to Nirvana; Nirvana being not a place of passion and sensual excitement so much as an oasis of peace, calm and predictability. She felt safe in

Nirvana, and feeling safe, as Hannah saw it, gave her the courage to now and again splash out, to venture to unknown places and, who knows, experience the odd moment of exhilaration – not the kind of immature, fleeting exhilaration of a new love affair, but something a lot more lasting, such as . . . she struggled to think of a for instance . . . Such as a remarkable piece of art on the wall of a gallery she'd never been to before, in an obscure part of London she didn't know. Or seeing spring daffodils for the first time in St James's Park. Silly things, maybe. The point was . . . She wasn't sure what the point was.

Her mind was seriously wandering.

He was charming, he was tender, he was loving – very loving. And they shared a long-ago history. He was also a rogue. He'd been a rogue all his life. But he made her laugh, and on many occasions in the past he'd made her cry. The conversation had been non-stop, wide-reaching, easy. She'd felt witty, and sexy, and intensely interesting. She'd told jokes and remembered the punchline. She'd asked questions without probing. She had sparkled, and the world had sparkled back. And when he hugged her she felt enveloped, cocooned, and terribly safe. They'd stood there together for minutes on end, locked into one another, her face buried in his neck, basking in the smell of him, feeling the gentle thrum of his heart, and she never never wanted that closeness to end.

Nirvana had gone now. Her oasis of quiet was no longer. Because from now on, she knew for certain no matter how much older she was, and supposedly wiser, she would be waiting for that phone to ring. Just like a teenager. And though he said he would ring her often from his home in Toronto – where he may or may not but probably did have a wife – and he would be over in London again in no time, she knew it was at best a fifty-fifty chance she'd ever hear from him again.

Meanwhile . . . There was little point now in seeking out those surprising little works of art in obscure galleries as they'd mean nothing if he wasn't with her. And what was the use of spending a glorious evening at the theatre if she could not share it with him? All those little life-support systems that had sustained her over the decades faded into insignificance, along with her friends. Along with everything.

It was ghastly, and it was glorious too.

She was well and truly fucked.

The spark

I remember every detail.

It was a late September morning, a soft sun, a beautiful day. I was ready. I had 'peaked' at exactly the right time: not too early and over-practised; not too late and under-prepared.

I wore my Madonna skirt over leggings. I was trend personified, with my crimped hair, clipped tidily back from my face, and my tailored jacket, sleek as a cat and looking older than my nineteen years, or so I fancied myself. Neat little low-heeled shoes, demure even, a careful mix of funk and sophistication.

It was up three flights. I half ran up those stairs, tap tap tap, feet clicking like castanets, into the little room at the top. It was a bare space, rough floorboards, just a piano and stool and in the corner, half hidden in the shadows, a grey-haired lady sitting behind a desk. She held a pencil in her hand.

'Moira Tay,' I said, panting slightly.

'Yes,' she said, smiling. 'Take your time.'

I did.

The window was open slightly, you could just hear the drone of traffic, a distant siren in F sharp. The swish of the breeze moving the curtains.

Concentrate.

I sat myself down, pulled the piano stool forwards and backwards a bit, the way I'd seen concert pianists do. Sat quietly counting out ten seconds, and then I began.

I played Chopin's *Nouvelle Étude No 3*. I played perfectly. I knew I would.

Everything was in place: timing, pace, dynamics, and above all rhythm. The left hand and the right, the one following split seconds after the other in relaxed and familiar harmony, like an echo. So difficult to do, so impossible to achieve. Achieved. Done. To perfection.

I felt transported, transcendent, lifted way above and beyond myself and my surroundings.

It was in the moment following.

'Thank you,' she said.

That's all. 'Thank you.' A downward inflection. A descending interval of a third. G to E. 'Thank you' – spoken quietly, sweetly even.

I sat there waiting – for what? For something more. She looked back at me, smiling still, head cocked slightly to one side, the pencil flicking back and forth between her fingers, like a metronome. She was waiting for me to leave.

In that moment, in that silence, I realised.

I had done my best, I had been perfect. And perfect was not enough. I was not going to make it as a concert pianist.

~

The girl was unprepossessing. She had a sullen expression and lank hair and she slouched. She was the reluctant daughter of aspirational parents, there had been plenty before like her. She resented being there. She resented everything – me, the music, the work, the world. She was withdrawn, negative and spotty. Even at that tender age – what would it have been, ten, eleven? – she was hunched, bent over like an old woman, as if she was trying to shrink from the world. Her fingers looked awkward on the keys, stiff and unnatural, and try as I did I could not make her relax them. We did exercises, trying to get her to loosen up, to hold her head up high (my mother's voice in my ear), look proud, pleased, happy to be alive, all that stuff. To no avail.

But then one day everything changed. I'd given her a Bach prelude, a particularly tricky one (is there any other sort?), thinking as I did so that this wasn't really fair, she couldn't be expected to come close, especially if she didn't practise.

My mind, as it tended to do, was drifting as she shuffled over to the piano, pulled the stool back and forth as she'd seen me do, laid her stiff little fingers on the keys and began to play.

Within seconds I was wide awake, upright in my chair with my mouth open. Those stiff little fingers that had defied everything I'd tried to teach her were running over the keys in their awkward little way with a fluency that took my breath away.

It was then that I realised there was something there, something extraordinary. Despite the wooden fingers and the sagging shoulders she had what I can only call the makings of a gift. You know, that's the part the teacher cannot teach, that you may only come upon once or twice in your life, or maybe never, but when it's there you recognise it, boy do you know when you see it. Or hear it.

My teachers had always drummed into me the importance of hard work. At school concerts there was the tiny tot on the violin, usually Chinese, who played way outside the possibilities for her age group, and when I asked the teacher how she got to be so talented he would simply say she worked harder than the rest of us. Which was true, undoubtedly, but that wasn't the point. 'Do you mean if I worked as hard as her I could be like her?' I'd asked, and he'd nod, barely looking at me, as if it was blindingly obvious.

But this girl. Hard work?

There's always someone in your class who gets better grades than you, than anyone, without appearing to put any work in at all. My mother used to tell me not to be envious, it wasn't something you'd wish on anyone, to find things so easy you didn't have to work for them. How else does a person get to appreciate anything? But this girl, her name was Rose, confounded all of them.

So I got to work on Rose. Leading by example I pulled myself up to my full height and I smiled, and adopted a bright expression, and I got her practising because I knew she had what I never had. She had the spark of genius.

It took a few years, but by the time she was fifteen or so I felt we were finally getting somewhere. Not only was she beginning to recognise her own talent she was showing signs of joining the world. She washed and crimped her hair, she smiled, she practised between classes and more than once I heard her laugh out loud. A year or so later she left me and went on to higher things. Other people had spotted her genius and so she enrolled in music college. The very same college I had failed in.

But she never did quite get the hang of the Chopin.

~

I slipped into the back of the Hall just before the concert began, as the lights went down. The stage was empty but for the grand piano, dramatically spotlit, majestic in the darkness. There was a hush and a slight pause, and then on she came.

She was wearing dark green velvet, low-cut, something sparkly around her neck. Her hair was crimped and clipped back from her face, a bit of a nineties look. She reminded me of someone. Oh yes, it was me. She bowed low and looked up at the gallery, like another teacher had taught her do. She sat down at the piano and pulled the stool this way and that. The audience waited. Then she began.

She played the Chopin *Nouvelle Etude* No 3, the piece I had tried to teach her. Played it in a way I had never heard it played before. Not as I had played it, not as I had taught it, but exactly as it was meant to sound: the left hand following the right a fraction of a second behind it, like a child running to keep up with the parent. That's how I had described it. The very same piece that had failed me, that I had perfected, thought I had perfected, she had made her own.

I felt I was hearing it for the first time.

She played with agonising restraint, toying with the tempo as she toyed with the audience's emotions. When it was over there was a stunned silence, and then the audience stood up and roared. After a moment she got slowly to her feet and remained there, by the piano, gazing about her, smiling graciously. Calm, confident, back as straight as a rod, graceful, beautiful and talented. A perfect cadence.

It was Rose's dream come true but it was mine as well. The spark I'd first identified all those years ago had burst into a radiant, glowing flame.

21st century woman (part 3)

ENDING

There were secret candlelit lunches,
There were passionate afternoons,
Romantic weekends in the country,
(Well one, anyway.)
It cost me a fortune in babysitting,
And eventually – my marriage.
But I didn't care,
I was happy.

It was a misty evening in April,
I was walking home with my lover,
When he kissed me and said – 'It's been great, my love,
But it's time to call it a day.'
And I cried, though I had no right to,
And I said as I tried to hold onto him:
'Please don't go, don't go – please stay – I'll do anything.'
(And I really said it that time.)

Twelve years as a wife,
Nine years as a mother,
A husband, a home and a family,

And look where I am today.
Here on a London pavement,
Thinking - how could I have thrown it away?
I wanted my cake,
And I choked on it.

I'm a 21st century woman,
Pragmatic and single-minded,
Got a career, a suit and a laptop,
I can hold my own in a boardroom.
But I'm afraid you'll have to forgive me,
'Cause I'm not the person I was.
Though loyalty
Once meant the world to me,
Now it's gone,
Flown
Right out of the window.

I'm a 21st century woman,
Mature and independent,
Got a brain, a degree and ambition,
Always knew where I was going.
But:
You no longer have to despise me,
'Cause I'm still the woman I was.
For the story you see – *thank God* –
Was just fantasy.
I'll get on with my boring old life
In a moment.

In the eye of the beholder

The following was first published in the Segora Anthology of poetry and short stories in 2010.

Rob spotted his older brother long before Victor spotted him. He'd been watching him in the mornings on his way to work, tap tapping down the street in that funny little mincing manner of his, looking neither to right nor left - it was the walk he recognised before anything else. From his position up there at fourth floor level Rob noticed, with some satisfaction, the beginnings of a bald patch right in the middle of his older brother's little round head.

They came face to face a couple of weeks later. The scaffolding was coming down and Rob was standing in the middle of the pavement in front of him. Victor came to a halt – he could hardly do otherwise – and stared at him for a moment, completely blank.

Then his eyes opened wide.

'Rob?' he said, with disbelief.

'Victor,' said Rob.

'What are you doing here?'

'What does it look like?'

Rob watched Victor's not-very-smart brain tick-ticking over, absorbing the shock – younger brother, in filthy clothes, standing by building site.

'You're working on a *building site*?' said Victor, eventually.

Rob smiled slightly.

There was an awkward little pause. Victor shifted from one foot to the other.

'I live round the corner,' he said.

'I know.'

'How do you know?'

'I've been watching you.'

Victor hesitated. Then, 'You should come and see it,' he said. 'Come now if you want.'

He wasn't sure why he said it. He wasn't sure if he wanted his younger brother anywhere near him, let alone in his private apartment.

'Okay.'

They walked down the street without saying a word to one another. Rob strolled, head down, hands in his pockets. He wore dirty loose trousers, a work shirt and a woolly hat, and he sauntered, as if he had all the time in the world. Victor had to slow down to keep pace with him. Victor was a busy man and he walked like a busy man, with short steps, laptop in right hand, busy, busy, busy, places to go, things to do. His brother's saunter irritated him. He found it disrespectful, even arrogant – that he, Victor, should be expected to walk at the same pace as his brother rather than the other way around.

They walked in silence. The two brothers who'd not spoken to one another in however long had nothing to say. And Rob, eyes on the pavement, did not invite conversation.

He was watching his brother out of the corner of his eye. He could see Victor was having difficulty keeping pace with him, struggling to slow himself down. It was ridiculous that walk of his. It was like a prissy little dance, on tippy-toes, his heels hardly touching the ground. It looked even more ludicrous now that his brother had grown a paunch, a prissy little paunch, that stretched the jacket of his suit and pulled it out of shape. He reminded Rob of an egg. Humpty-Dumpty.

They reached Victor's block of flats and walked in, still in silence. Victor held the door for his brother and in he strolled, hands still in pockets. They took the lift to the fifth floor.

'I think you're going to like this.' Why did he say that? Was he looking for approval? Yet Victor couldn't resist a tiny flourish as he opened the door to his apartment and ushered in his younger brother.

Rob strolled into the middle of the living room and looked around.

He saw a huge painting above the fireplace – a woman doing something or other with a swan. A bare wood floor covered in small rugs, lots of them, in weird shapes and colours. A picture window. Some tables made out of dark wood. Two massive sofas, one of them a sort of plum colour and the other a dark purple – in fact there was a lot of pink in the room now he came to look at it, which made Rob stop and think for a bit. The walls, at least, were normal, magnolia probably, they were the only normal things in the room. It looked like something out of House and Garden only artier.

'Very nice,' he said.

Very *nice?* Victor frowned.

Rob took off his beanie and pushed his hand through his mass of thick, golden, unruly hair. Rather provocatively, thought Victor, resisting the urge to run his own hand over his own bald patch.

'Can I touch it?' The little boy stretched out a hand to his brother.

'Get off me!'

'I only wanted to touch your hair!'

Just to see if it was real. Real gold.

'Do you mind taking off your shoes?' said Victor.

'Okay.' Rob did so, holding onto the back of an upright chair to steady himself, and then making a bit of a pantomime of tiptoeing across the room to place his boots carefully upon the doormat well out of harm's way.

'So, what do you think?'

'It's . . .' Rob nodded again. 'Yeah.'

'It's professionally designed. I hired a guy, told him the effect I was looking for and he did the rest. That's a limited edition Mackelthorpe,' Victor pointed to the painting above the fireplace.

There was a pause.

'Mackelthorpe? You know him? Nineties. Long-listed for the Turner 1997, or very nearly.'

'Right.'

'And the rugs are from China, of course. Hand-embroidered.'

'Yeah well it's all very . . .' Rob sucked air through his teeth. A disgusting habit from childhood.

'All very what?'

'You know. All very House and Garden.'

Victor glared at his brother. His expression was blank, bland. Okay, so he was unimpressed. Or determined to appear so.

'Sit down.' Victor spoke rather peremptorily. 'And tell me what you've been up to. Oh, hang on . . .'

He disappeared from the room and reappeared immediately with a towel, which he quickly placed under his brother's descending bottom.

'No offence, but you know.'

'Chinese again?'

'These sofas? No, they're Italian.'

So Victor sat on one sofa and his brother sat on the other, with a towel under him, and the two brothers stared at one another across the chasm of Victor's spacious apartment and who knows how many years of sibling estrangement.

'So.' Victor didn't want to have to be the first to speak but he found the silence excruciating. 'You're working on a building site. Why?'

His brother stared back at him. He had these – penetrating, there was no other word for it – blue eyes. Beautiful. Women loved them.

'Those eyes. He is going to be a stunner when he's older, isn't he dad?'

'I'll say. We're going to have to keep an eye on him mum.'

'Why not?' was the answer.

Victor sighed. He should have known better than to have asked.

Rob saw the flash of annoyance on his brother's face. He felt a tiny pang of regret.

'It suits me,' he said, with a hint of a smile. 'How about you?'

'Well, I haven't done too badly.' Victor wriggled his round little frame into the ample cushions of his Carpacciani sofa. He loved the way they gave way under his weight and softly settled themselves around his frame and held him, just like he dreamed of his mum doing.

Rob watched his elder brother disappearing into the ludicrously over-stuffed cushions of some Italian designer's wet fantasy. He pictured him as a character in a Roald Dahl novel, being slowly swallowed and sucked into the sofa until there was nothing left of him but his little round, balding head.

'Are you still working for the bank?' asked Rob.

'No, I'm in futures.'

'Oh yeah?'

Victor saw his brother's lip curl, slightly. He doesn't have a clue what I'm talking about, he thought, but he sneers anyway.

Then quite suddenly, and with a little bit of effort – the Carpacciano sofa did not release its prisoners easily – Victor emerged from the Italian pinkness and stood up.

'I've got a fantastic view over London, would you like to see it?'

And before Rob could reply Victor was pressing a button on the wall and hey presto, the picture window was gliding open – *hummmmm* - and he was stepping out onto some sort of balcony.

'The Heath,' Victor pointed. 'And beyond it the Royal Free, monstrous building. And over there . . .' he waited as Rob joined him. 'The Cheesegrater, Canary Wharf, the Shard – every London landmark, right there before your eyes. And those there are the whatever-they-are, the South Downs? Right across London, can you believe it?'

Rob just nodded.

'Over in that direction, just around there, between those two tall buildings, you can actually see the Mall. Or rather, you can see where it is, the fly-pasts, you know? The Red Arrows? When there's a fly-past you can see them perfectly flying from left to right, east to west, on the dot. It's amazing. You know . . .' He paused for a moment, leaning on the rail at the edge of his roof terrace. 'At times I feel proud to be British.'

'Huh?'

Victor pulled out a handkerchief and blew into it loudly. 'Some years ago, the Queen's – what was it, her golden jubilee? There was a fly-past, and things were running late, and I was thinking to myself – what about the Red Arrows, they have to take off from wherever it is, miles away – how do they time it? What if they're early? It's not as if they can quietly circle overhead waiting for the right moment. But would you believe it! Bang! There they were, out of the blue, literally. Bang on time. To the second. Total precision.' He sniffed into his handkerchief. 'I get quite emotional just thinking about it,' he said.

There was no response. He looked, and there was no one there.

Rob was standing in the middle of the living room, yawning and stretching.

Victor took a deep breath. It had happened again. He had allowed it to happen again.

He went back inside the flat. *Hummmmm* . . . the patio doors closed behind him.

'Well Rob,' he said, as politely as he could, 'it's been good seeing you.'

'Huh?' Rob swung round. 'Are you throwing me out?'

What Victor really wanted was to give his brother a hug. A big bear hug.

'Keep your hands off me, you pervert!'

'I'm not a pervert! Can't I hug my baby brother?'

All he wanted was some of his glitter to rub off on him. He had plenty to spare.

And even now, in his filthy work clothes . . .

'I worked for all this you know,' is what he said.

Rob stared at him. Blank eyes. Beautiful, but blank.

'I worked fucking hard. I didn't start out with anything, you know.'

'I do know. I was there, remember?'

'This – all this – is my own work. And I'm fucking proud of it. You on the other hand . . .' He stopped.

'I on the other hand?'

'Don't forget your shoes.'

But don't go. I don't want you to. Just – hug me. Give me validation.

'Okay, hint taken.'

Rob ruffled his hair once again, in bewilderment. His brother . . . couldn't make him out at all. One moment he seemed desperate to impress, the next . . . fuck it, he came here didn't he? He didn't have to. He didn't have to show himself in the first place.

He shuffled in his socked feet towards the door.

'When did you last see mum and dad?' asked Victor suddenly.

Rob sighed. 'I wondered when you'd get round to that.'

'They ask about you.' He didn't want to give his baby brother the satisfaction of knowing that every single time he, Victor, visited his parents - which was often, once a month at least, and it was an effort to go all that way - they did nothing else but talk about him. About Rob, the absent one, the one made all that more conspicuous and interesting because of his absence, from all their lives.

'Have you heard from him?'

'Not a thing.'

'We do worry.'

'I shouldn't. He can take care of himself.'

'But he was so – vulnerable. He was always the vulnerable one of the two of you.'

'They worry about you,' Victor said.

Rob nodded. He bent down to pick up his shoes. And in that moment, the moment before he picked them up, or even quite possibly in the moment after, because the door was still closed, the moment was still there, the opportunity . . .

Let's not do this.

Let's not part on these terms.

Please hug me.

Victor opened the door and with a nod, Rob walked through it.

'See you,' he said.

'See you.'

~

Victor walked back through his French doors – *hummm*

140

– onto his roof terrace. The sun was low in the sky, to his right. He observed its glow on the sides of the buildings, the lengthening of the shadows on the roofs, the flash of its reflection on a pane of glass on a Canary Wharf building. Up here you could feel omnipotent. Up here you could play at being Phoebus, pulling the sun across the sky in his golden chariot and then racing around the back, the dark side, in time to begin all over again the following morning.

He looked down at the street, at the toy cars, the pretend people. He saw his brother emerge from the building and head off down the street, hands in pockets, head bowed, not so much sauntering, it looked to Victor now, as slouching.

Shakespeare revisited

In idle moments I like to rewrite the lyrics to well-known songs, or in this case the words of famous sonnets, Shakespeare's in particular. Here is one of them: the original followed by mine.

SONNET 138

When my love swears that she is made of truth,
I do believe her though I know she lies,
That she might think me some untutored youth,
Unlearnèd in the world's false subtleties.
Thus vainly thinking that she thinks me young,
Although she knows my days are past the best,
Simply I credit her false-speaking tongue;
On both sides thus is simple truth suppressed.
But wherefore says she not she is unjust,
And wherefore say not I that I am old?
O, love's best habit is in seeming trust,
And age in love loves not to have years told.
Therefore I lie with her, and she with me,
And in our faults by lies we flattered be.

MY VERSION

When my love swears I am the only one,
I do believe him, though I know he lies.
That he might think me, when all's said and done,
A pretty special person in his eyes.
Thus vainly thinking that he misses me -
When out of sight I know is out of mind -
Simply that makes me an accessory:
On both sides thus is simple truth maligned.
But wherefore says he not he is untrue?
And wherefore say not I that I'm deceived?
Why, thus he has his cake and eats it too,
But given love means more than love received.
Therefore I lie with him and him with me,
Equal partners both in duplicity.

Reasons for living

'How are you dad?'

'Bloody awful.'

'I'm sorry to hear that.'

'It's time I buggered off. If you had any love for me you'd stick a pillow over my head.'

'Yeah, well, sorry dad, but that's not on the cards.'

'Don't see why not. What's the point?'

'The point of what?'

'Anything.'

Peter did not answer that.

'Why am I still alive? Tell me that.'

'Why are any of us alive?'

'It's all right for you, you can get about. You've got a family. What have I got? I'm just a half-witted, half-crippled idiot. No use to anyone. Reached my sell-by.'

There was a pause.

Father, looking admittedly pretty raddled, his hair unbrushed, face unshaven, was sitting on the side of his bed, in his pyjamas. His son stood close by, looking down at him.

'Well? What do you have to say about that?' he said.

'Dad, I've arranged for a new carer to come in.'

'Huh? What's that? A new carer? What for?'

'Because none of the old carers will have a bar of you.'

'See? I told you so. No use to anyone.'

'It's one thing being abusive to your own family. But when people are trying to help you, people you don't know, there's no need to take it out on them.'

His middle-aged son, whose name was Peter, was a decent man, if fundamentally unremarkable. He'd always had a sticky relationship with his father, ever since he was a kid. Now that his dad was more or less totally dependent on him did not make things any easier. There was very little he said these days that Peter had not heard before, many times over.

'They're useless, all of them,' his father was saying. 'Turn up late. Call me Des – not even Desmond, not even Mr Desmond, let alone Mr Berryman. And they don't speak a word of English, half of them.'

'They're doing their best, dad. If you want them to call you Mr Berryman you have to tell them that. They're just trying to be friendly.'

'Friendly? You call that friendly? I call it over-familiarity. No respect.'

The old man shifted in his bed. The bed he rarely got out of these days, except for the necessary.

'The new carer is from Jamaica, dad. She's called Blessing.' Peter pulled up a chair and sat down. Clearly this was going to take longer than he'd hoped.

'Blessing?' The old man snorted. 'She's not a darkie, is she?' He turned his aggressive gaze onto his mild-mannered son.

'Yes, dad, she is a darkie, as you call it.'

'I'm not having a darkie in my house.'

'Don't call her a darkie. And you have no choice. As I said, the council people won't come any more, you've been black-listed.'

'"Black-listed?"'

'So, frankly, you have no choice. You can't manage on

your own.'

'Stick a pillow over my head. Now. Go on son. Get it over with. What's the point?'

'Stop feeling so sorry for yourself. Stop saying what's the point? I am not sticking a pillow over your head. To begin with it's illegal . . .'

'Ah. You're worried you'll go to prison for it.'

'It's called murder, dad.'

'It's called mercy killing, son.'

'I can't do it. I won't do it.'

'Give me one good reason. Other than you going to prison. You'd get off. Plenty of people have done it before you.'

Again Peter did not reply. He gazed miserably at his clasped hands. He knew his father was staring at him and he did not want to return the stare.

'So tell me son, what's the point? Eh? Answer me that. What's the point of an old codger like me going on living, eh? I can't do anything. The only thing I can do is make people's lives a misery. Yours included. Yours especially. So what do you have to say to that?'

Peter sighed. He stood up and replaced the chair next to the wall.

'As I said, her name's Blessing, dad. She has a key. She'll be here 9 o'clock in the morning.'

'I'm not having a darkie in my house.'

'Well there's not much you can do about it. And you be civil to her, do you hear? Because this is your last chance.'

'"Last chance", eh?' The old man laughed, and then coughed. He was still coughing when his son left the house.

~

'I don't want you here.'

'Why not, Desmond?'

'And I'm not having you call me Desmond. My name is

Mr Berryman.'

'I beg your pardon, Mr Berryman. My name is Blessing. Please tell me why you don't want me here.'

The old man did not reply.

'Is it to do with the colour of my skin by any chance?'

'It's very personal. What you're doing is very personal. I want a man to do it.'

'I'm sorry but there are no male carers available, not from my agency. There are not many male carers in the business at all.'

'What are you doing?'

'I'm trying to get you out of bed.'

'Not that way! Stupid woman, what are you trying to do?'

'Then tell me how to do it.'

'You lift me here, under the armpit.'

'Right.'

'Like that. No, not like that!'

'I'm sorry.'

'You're too rough! I'm an old man.'

'I am aware of that.'

'Anyway I don't need a bath. I had a bath just the other day. My son did it. He's cack-handed as hell but we get there.'

'Your son is busy. He has work to do, and he's not here now.'

'No! Don't pull me!'

'Then tell me how you want me to get you out of bed.'

'I can do it myself.'

'Very well. Then let's see you do it.'

The young woman stood back as the old man first heaved himself upright, and then, bit by bit, he shuffled his backside to the edge of the bed and, with great and noisy effort, he swung first one leg and then the other over the side of the bed until both feet were on the floor.

'Well done!' said Blessing.

'Don't you "well done" me, young woman,' said the old man. He was panting with effort.

'Do you need help getting to your feet?'

'Yes. No! Don't touch me!'

'I have to touch you sooner or later.'

'I won't have a darkie touching me.'

'I am afraid you'll have to get used to that.'

The old man tried to stand up. With his bum on the bed and both feet on the floor, he managed to push himself off until he was half upright, where he paused, shaking slightly, and panting. The young woman continued to stand there, watching him but making no attempt to help.

'Christ Almighty, give me a hand.'

She went to grab him under the armpits. He screamed.

'What's the matter?'

'I said don't touch me!'

'I cannot give you a hand without touching you.'

'Get your nigger hands off me!'

'If I take my hands off you you will fall down.'

'I . . . I . . .' The old man yelped with pain again. He stood there, shaking, the woman's hands still holding him. He took a small step and steadied himself.

'That's better. Now you have your balance.'

The young woman removed one hand from the old man's armpit.

'It's a shocking state of affairs. What's the point?'

'The point of what?'

'The point! The bloody point! Of anything. Of me . . .' the old man winced, and nearly over-balanced. The young woman was still holding onto him. 'All this. What's the point?'

'Well, the point is to get you to the bathroom and all spruced up.'

'Spruced up? What for, eh? What the hell for? Who do I

want to get spruced up for, eh?'

'For me. And for yourself. Steady now.'

The young woman held him by the arm as he shuffled towards the bathroom.

'I'm going to wet myself.'

'No you're not. We're nearly there. You can make it.'

'I'm going to wet myself and there's nothing you can do about it.'

'All right, go ahead, if that's what you want.'

But he didn't. For the last few paces he managed to quicken up. They made it to the bathroom just in time. She whipped down his trouser bottoms just as he reached the toilet and sank heavily onto the seat.

As he peed he sighed with relief.

'Well done,' said the young woman.

'Bugger off,' said the old man.

~

'How was it?'

'How was what?'

'Blessing. You and Blessing. How did you get on?'

'She's a ruddy nuisance. She's rough as hell. And she tried to call me Desmond.'

'She speaks English at least.'

'That's about all you can say for her.'

They were together again, father and son, in the bedroom. Dad on the bed, looking not quite so raddled this time.

'You're looking pretty good. Better than you've looked for some time.'

'Well I'm not feeling it.'

'She shaved you, did she?'

'I didn't ask her to do that. She doesn't listen to a word I say.'

'That's probably just as well. You didn't call her a darkie, I hope.'

'So what if I did?'

'It's racist, dad. It's insulting, and it's unnecessary.'

'She doesn't seem to mind.'

'You don't know that. She was probably just being polite. It's hurtful.'

'It's true. She is a darkie.'

'Anyway, by the looks of it she's done you a power of good.'

The old man grunted. 'She's not coming again, is she?'

'Of course she is. She's coming every day, you know that.'

'I won't have a darkie in my house.'

'You've had what you call a darkie in your house, dad, and she's done marvels on you. The only question is, will she agree to come again, if you insist on insulting her?'

'I don't want her coming here. What's the point?'

'If you say "what's the point" one more time, I'll . . .' The young man stopped.

'You'll what? Throttle the life out of me? Go on, I dare you!' The old man stretched out his neck. Then he sank back into his pillows and laughed, and the laugh turned to coughing. He was still coughing when his son left the house.

~

'Go on, eat something.'

'I'm not hungry.'

'You have to eat something.'

'Why? What's the point?'

'I cooked it for you specially.'

'It's none of your Jamaican rubbish, is it?'

'It's sausages and mash. Your son tells me it's your favourite.'

'What would he know?'

'Go on, please. It'll make you feel better.'

'I don't want to feel better.'

'You don't want to feel better? What sort of talk is that?'

'What's the point?'

'What's the point of what?'

'Anything.'

'What's the point of anything? Do things have to have a point?'

'Everyone has to have a reason to get up in the morning.'

'Do they? I never heard that before.'

'Why do you get up in the morning?'

'I never gave it a thought. I get up in the morning because I have things to do.'

'There you are then. You have things to do. What about the likes of us? We have nothing to do. So what's the point of getting up in the morning?'

'Of course you can't do things if you're lying in bed all day.'

'There you are then.'

'Go on, eat up. It's getting cold.'

The old man lay back in his bed for a moment. Then he said: 'I want to get up.'

'What, now?'

'Yes, now.'

'All right. I'll just pop your plate back in the kitchen. We can warm it up in the microwave. You do have a microwave, do you?'

'What do you think I am?'

'I meant nothing by it.'

Blessing disappeared briefly into the kitchen and was back in a trice. Oh!' she said.

'What?'

'You managed it by yourself. Getting out of bed. That was quick.'

He was standing by his bed, shaking slightly, hanging

on to the bedhead.

'Let me help you.'

'I don't need your help.'

'Very well.'

Once again the young woman watched as the old man made his way unsteadily towards the armchair. He stood before it for several moments, as if thinking what to do next. He reached out and placed his hands on the arms of the chair and then he stopped. Blessing stood, still watching him, her arms folded.

Then with a sudden and wildly uncontrolled movement the old man twisted himself around and fell into the chair, sideways, nearly missing it altogether, but not quite. The young woman continued watching as he wriggled his bottom further into the seat. Then he laughed, and coughed a bit.

'Excellent,' said Blessing. 'Now are you ready for your food?'

'As ready as I'll ever be,' said Desmond.

~

'Are you married?'

'Yes I am.'

'Kids?'

'Yes, two girls.'

'You're lucky. I've only got boys.'

'Why is it luckier to have girls than boys?'

'They look after you when you're old.'

'Ah.'

'I expect your husband buggered off, did he? Like all those darkies? I suppose you're a single mum, like the rest of them.'

'No. As a matter of fact my husband didn't "bugger off like the rest of them" as you put it. How's the temperature?'

'The what?'

'The temperature, of the water, is it okay?'

'It's too hot.'

'All right, that's easily fixed.'

'Why do you do this job then, if you have a husband?'

'The money is useful. And I enjoy it.'

'You enjoy looking after people like me, do you? You must be desperate.'

'How is it now?'

'What?'

'The water.'

'It's all right.'

'I like caring for people. It's a useful thing to do. I like to be useful.'

'You make a lot of money out of it, do you?'

'Hardly. The agency takes a big chunk. It just about covers my bus fare. And the school uniforms. And a little bit over.'

'I don't understand why you put up with it. Why you put up with me. With the likes of me.'

'You know you have surprisingly soft skin.'

'Who, me? Ow!'

'Sorry.'

'You're too rough.'

'It's because your skin is so thin. That's partly why it's so soft. And very sensitive.'

'That tickles.'

'Does it now?'

'Stop it!'

'Sorry, I couldn't resist.'

'You're too cheeky for your own good, did you know that?'

'I did apologise.'

'Well just don't do it again.'

'On one condition.'

'What's that?'

'You stop calling me a darkie.'

'What's wrong with calling you a darkie? You are a darkie. You're not ashamed of it are you?'

'Far from it. But it is an offensive word.'

'What do you prefer then? Nigger? Black? Negro? Blimey, how are you supposed to know what's right and what isn't right these days? It's political correctness gone mad.'

'The correct word, so-called, is 'people of colour'. Or 'person of colour', in this case. But frankly I don't see that it's necessary. My name is Blessing, I'm happy to go by that name. My parents were from Jamaica, so I am also Jamaican. As far as I am concerned my skin colour is not relevant.'

'You can't say a skin colour isn't relevant. It's blindingly obvious. Staring at you in the face. Literally.'

'Would you like to wash yourself down there or shall I do it for you?'

'Give it me.' Desmond snatched the sponge from Blessing's fingers and dabbed delicately at his private parts. 'When I was a youngster there weren't any darkies. "People of colour". People like you. They just didn't exist.'

The young woman did not respond to this. When he had finished his most intimate ablutions she took the sponge from him and gently washed his back and his neck. Desmond closed his eyes.

'It is a changing world.'

'Who'd have thought it. At my age. I'd find myself sitting in a bath while a black woman washed my neck!'

'Lucky you,' she said.

'Don't you be so sure,' said Desmond.

~

'What do you mean you don't want her back?'

'She's cheeky,' said Desmond.

'Cheeky? What's wrong with that? You mean she

overstepped the mark?'

'And she took advantage.'

'How?'

'In the bath. She touched my private parts. Without asking permission.'

Peter laughed, despite himself. 'She was probably just washing you. What else is she supposed to do?'

'She touched me. Inappropriately,' the old man insisted.

His son looked at his father quizzically. 'Then we'd better have a word with her,' he said. 'If you feel she was touching you up inappropriately. That's a serious allegation.'

'Yes,' said his father.

'It is a fine line,' said Peter. 'Bathing someone is a very intimate business. I don't think carers, or nurses for that matter, look on it in the same way we do. It's just a job for them. A body is just a body. Besides . . .' he snorted. 'It's not as if yours is exactly desirable!' He tried not to laugh but couldn't help himself.

'Go on, laugh away.'

'You know dad, you are ridiculous sometimes.'

'I don't want that nigger in the house again.'

'So it's "nigger" now, is it? I trust you didn't call her that to her face.'

'I may have done. It was no more than she deserved.'

'So you do acknowledge it is an offensive word. That's something anyway.'

The old man just grunted.

~

'I told them I didn't want you in the house again.'

'I heard,' said Blessing.

'Then what are you doing here?'

'I asked myself the same thing.' She removed her coat and hung it on the hatstand in the hallway. Desmond was up and about, and watching her.

'And I came to the conclusion,' she went on, dabbing at her hair, 'that you would actually be lost without me. I could not desert you.'

'Lost? What, you mean like the sheep? You're not a God-botherer, are you? Like the rest of your sort?'

'As a matter of fact I'm not. Unlike my parents. You are up and about, I see.'

'Well that's very observant of you.'

'You found a reason to get up this morning then?'

The old man shrugged. 'You know as well as I do,' said Blessing, 'that I am the only one who can put up with you. Your son told me as much. I was warned, you see. And as for that ridiculous accusation of touching you inappropriately . . .' she looked at him, frowning gently, like a teacher with a recalcitrant child, 'what sort of nonsense was that?'

'That was true,' said Desmond.

'Well, let's just ignore it, shall we? For the time being? But please don't do it again, it is hurtful, and unfair.'

'What would you know about unfair?'

'A great deal, as it happens.'

'Poor you,' said the old man disdainfully. And he turned and made to walk back into his bedroom.

'You're not getting back into bed, are you?'

'Why, what's it to you?'

'It's everything to me. You got yourself up this morning, without prompting, and without help. And now you're going to go back on everything and climb back into your bed! What sort of behaviour is that?'

'I will tell you.' He stopped in the doorway and all but spat at her. 'It's what I want to do! Don't talk to me about behaviour, as if I was a child! What sort of a word is behaviour anyway?'

'I am sorry.' She spoke sincerely. 'It was wrong of me, I

apologise.'

'I should think so.' He continued to stand there, in the doorway of his bedroom.

'I know it is far too easy to treat the elderly like children, I apologise. It's not something I normally do. Even though,' she added, with the hint of a smile, 'let's face it you do behave like children at times, some of you.'

They stood still for a moment. She in the hallway, he on the threshold of his bedroom. He was scowling at her, she was smiling at him.

'What happens now?' she said.

He grunted.

'Breakfast? Did you eat breakfast yet?'

'No.'

'Right. So that is what happens now.'

And she walked into the kitchen.

~

To Peter's surprise she came to the funeral. She was dressed for it, all in black, with a hat, unlike the rest of the family who seemed to turn up in whatever they happened to be wearing that day.

'He invited me,' she explained.

'Who did, dad?'

She nodded. 'He made a point of it. "That'll show them", he said.'

'Show who?'

She shrugged. 'The family, I presume. He didn't say.'

Peter frowned. 'I don't get it. He was awful to you.'

'He was awful to everyone, from what you told me.'

'But you especially, because of . . .' he stopped.

'My colour? I know that. I knew that. He was not the only one. I am used to it, it doesn't bother me. It bothered me less than it bothered him.'

There was a pause. A strange thought was beginning to form in Peter's mind.

'Did he ever . . .' he began. 'I mean, as time went on, did it get better? Between you?'

'Absolutely.'

'It did? In what way?'

'Well, the insults never stopped. In some ways they got worse. He was testing me I think.'

'So?'

'He got himself out of bed in the mornings, before I arrived mostly.'

Peter scratched his head. 'You're saying he got out of bed – he found a reason to get out of bed – in order to insult you?'

'That's putting it rather simplistically. Let's say he was motivated, to do bad or to do good, it didn't matter.'

'To spite you?'

'Maybe. It doesn't matter.'

'He used to say to me, "What's the point?" To everything. "What's the point?" And there was no answer to it. I couldn't think what to say, because quite honestly there wasn't any point. Not really. Not that either of us could think of. And he knew that.'

'I don't think he had ever had a conversation with a black woman before. It was strange for him. But I like to think that by the end . . .' she paused.

'Yes?'

'He was used to me. He realised I was not so very different to him, in many ways.'

'So that. Was the point.'

Blessing smiled. 'You could say,' she said.

A helluva last night out

When Moses turns up on the back doorstep crack of dawn this morning my first thought is, *Well, has he been out on the town or what?*

He's leaning against the doorframe and giving me the eye in a skewed kind of way as, now I look closely at him, the other one looks the worse for wear. He's only been allowed out of the house on his own for a couple of weeks and he's been gone for three days and I'd all but given up on him. So my second thought is, *This guy need a chaperone.* After all you wouldn't let your kids out and about on their own until they're, what, on their way to being teenagers, would you?

I pick him up and he gives me a look that's a mix of world-weary and smug, as if to say, *You'll never guess in a million years where I've been*, and I'm telling him boy, you can say that again. And as I set about looking for his box to take him to the vet for a once-over I begin to imagine exactly what he *has* been up to.

He probably started out over the road at Mrs Lester's, as she has these curtains, brocade or something, with stubbly bits all over. And boy does Moses love to get his claws into Mrs Lester's curtains. Once he's done giving them a good shred he'll make for her sofa and scratch himself silly on the corner of it – all the stuff he knows he can't get away with at home. Mrs Lester being what you might call a soft touch doesn't seem to mind, not one bit, she'll even put out a saucer of milk for him and he'll devour that as if he's *starving*, as if his owners, the skinflints, never give him a thing to eat or drink from dawn to dusk.

Next he'd have headed off down Market Street, it being Friday the day he went missing, and I reckon he'd have picked up an *hors d'oeuvre* from Danny the fish – halibut maybe, or a bit of plaice – Danny being also a soft touch, they're everywhere in our neighbourhood.

From there, belly full and happy as a pig in shit Moses'd be looking around for some action, it being getting dark and so on. He'll have headed downtown, following the lights – he's no fool is Moses, even though as I said he's only been allowed outside for a couple of weeks – and he'd have showed up at the Lion and Unicorn and terrorised their dog Scruffy, who thinks he's the big I Am except when it comes to Moses. Then just to pay his respects to Scruffy's owner our Mo'd have headed out the back and hunted down a rat – there's always plenty of them hanging around the bins – and he'd have picked it up by the scruff and deposited it right in the middle of the pub on a Friday night when it's as crowded as hell, just to see how many minutes it takes to empty the space.

Then full of the joys Moses'll have carried on down the high street as far as the Yankee. On a Friday night there'll be a queue stretching round the block, but Moses'd have shot right past and headed inside when no one was looking. Friday nights is cabaret night, as they call it, though it's lap-dancing really – so I've heard, I wouldn't know it myself. He'd have found himself a ringside seat and ordered himself a cocktail and watched the show, and afterwards if he'd given her the glad-eye he'd have had the blonde one, the one with the legs that go up to here, and he'd have curled up on her lap, if she had one, as Moses wouldn't quite get it that lap dancing means the girl gets to sit on the guy's lap, not the other way around. Afterwards they'd have gone back to her place, maybe stopping off at Romy's the all-nighter for a nightcap, and then he's all set to conk out on her sofa, which is deep and soft and smothered in cushions with dangly bits on them so he has something to fiddle with through the night if he can't sleep.

There are marks down Moses's back, so maybe the girl had a cat of her own, one that won't have any other cats on their territory, you know the sort. That's probably where he lost his eye, in the fight. His back leg on the right hand side isn't working properly either, so I reckon the scrap left him the worse for wear and what with the blind eye and the wonky leg he must have had a close encounter with a lamppost, or maybe – the vet's saying now there's internal damage, he doesn't know the extent of it, not yet – maybe something a bit heavier, and moveable, like something travelling along the street at speed that Moses, being still a youngster, doesn't quite have the hang of yet.

The vet's telling me now the internal damage is pretty bad so he thinks it would be kinder to Moses to have him put down, because a cat like that wouldn't want to live a half life, not one like Moses. So I'm having to say okay, you're the boss, you do what's right, though it comes out all choky, as I guess you don't know till you're about to lose something how precious that something is, even if he is still a youngster.

He goes gently, drifting off to sleep right there on the vet's operating table, as quietly as you like, didn't feel a thing the vet said. And I'm thinking to myself it's a shame, he was quite a character as cats go, was Moses, he had a short life but a merry one. But he can rest easy knowing he had one helluva last night out.

Author biography

Patsy Trench began her working life as an actress, in the UK and in Australia, where she briefly lived in her twenties. She has worked as a scriptwriter for television, theatre and radio, then as a script editor, playscout and literary manager. She co-founded The Children's Musical Theatre of London, creating devised musicals with young children, and she has written lyrics for cabaret songs and for the grownup musical *IT*. In normal circumstances (pre-Covid) she organises theatre tours for overseas visitors to London and teaches and lectures on theatre. The mother of two adult children and one grandson she lives in north London and has a Freedom Pass.

Also by Patsy Trench

Non fiction

Australia: a personal story series
The Worst Country in the World (2012)
A Country To Be Reckoned With (2018)
Australia and How To Find It (2019)

Fiction

Modern Women: The Roaring Twenties series
The Awakening of Claudia Faraday (2019)
The Purpose of Prudence de Vere (2019)

Modern Women: Entertaining Edwardians
The Makings of Violet Frogg (2021)
Mrs Morphett's Macaroons (2021)

Social media

Facebook: https://www.facebook.com/PatsyTrenchWriting
Twitter: https://twitter.com/PatsyTrench
Instagram:
https://www.instagram.com/claudiafaraday1920

Website: https://patsytrench.com/